LOST WORLD

PATRÍCIA MELO is a novelist, scriptwriter and playwright. Her previous novels *The Killer*, *In Praise of Lies*, *Inferno* and *Black Waltz* are all published by Bloomsbury. In 1999, *Time* magazine included her among the fifty 'Latin American Leaders for the New Millennium'. She lives in São Paulo and in Switzerland.

CLIFFORD E. LANDERS has translated from Brazilian Portuguese novels by such writers as Rubem Fonseca, Jorge Amado, João Ubaldo Ribeiro, Jô Soares, Chico Buarque, and José de Alencar as well as shorter fiction by Lima Barreto, Rachel de Queiroz, Osman Lins and Moacyr Scliar. He received the Mario Ferreira Award in 1999 and a translation grant from the National Endowment for the Arts in 2004. His *Literary Translation: A Practical Guide* was published by Multilingual Matters Ltd in 2001.

LOST WORLD

Patrícia Melo

Translated from the Brazilian Portuguese
by Clifford Landers

BLOOMSBURY

LONDON · BERLIN · NEW YORK · SYDNEY

First published in Great Britain 2009
This paperback edition published 2010

Copyright © 2009 by Patrícia Melo
Translation copyright © by Clifford Landers 2009

Bloomsbury Publishing Plc
36 Soho Square
London W1D 3QY

www.bloomsbury.com

Bloomsbury Publishing, London, New York and Berlin

A CIP catalogue record for this book is available from the British Library

ISBN 978 1 4088 0115 4

10 9 8 7 6 5 4 3 2 1

Typeset by Hewer Text UK Ltd, Edinburgh
Printed in Great Britain by Clays Ltd, St Ives plc

FSC
www.fsc.org
MIX
Paper from
responsible sources
FSC® C018072

To Luiza

I

I'm a fugitive. And there were a lot of people at the cemetery. Where did all those blacks come from? I was uneasy, I didn't go closer. A bunch of blacks, two girls in shorts, I COULD CARE LESS printed on the T-shirt of one of them. I don't like commotion. I avoid it as much as possible. That's my way. I'm a fugitive.

The secret, said a guy who hid me when I ran away from São Paulo, the secret if you don't want to get caught is not to be seen with more than three. Or by yourself. And if you are by yourself, carry a newspaper under your arm, they'll think you're legit. To him, there was no problem if you got on packed trains, walked down crowded avenues, if everybody saw you there: Everybody is nobody, he said. No problem with hordes, as long as you stay away from football stadiums and funk dances, which are complications for sure. In Brazil, he said, there's no shame in having an

1

arrest warrant out against you. It's all the same, poor, rich, white, the hotshots, I mean cabinet members, council men, bigwigs, everybody's got one. Brazilians are like that, real scumbags. It's part of our culture to steal, to play dirty. It's like being a hold-up victim: sooner or later everybody is. And there's so many thieves, crooks, sons of bitches, killers, con artists, forgers that they can't put 'em all in jail. There's not enough space. So we get a free pass. It's just a matter of not calling attention to yourself, being invisible, keeping cool, know what I mean? Don't get in an accident, and don't go running around at night with black people. Because they go after blacks first. It's a tradition. And always have a woman with you. That helps a lot. And now the most important thing, when you get up every morning, repeat out loud: I'm a fugitive.

I don't know if the guy followed his own rules, but I heard he got caught.

I stayed there, in the distance, under the sun, watching the gravedigger bury my aunt. Itching to get out of there. I didn't know she had so many friends. Then I was relieved to see that the blacks were there for a burial at the neighboring grave. The girls in shorts too. Even more people showed up when the deceased arrived, wheeled by family members. I can't take it, said a blonde, when they lowered the casket. Blondes are very dramatic.

Aunt Rosa's funeral was suddenly empty, just five people. I don't count, I stayed back as a precaution. I'm a fugitive.

Right away I recognized her neighbor, Divani. You must be Máiquel, she'd said the day before.

I was in the living room, going through the plastic bag with Aunt Rosa's things the nurse at the hospital had given me. Bible, brand-new lipstick, pocketbook, documents, coin purse, cellphone, a small photo of my cousin Robinson, rusty hairpins, address book, plumber's card, a crumpled-up packet of aspirin, shit, it broke my heart to see those things, all tossed together in a bag. That was when Divani invaded the house.

Pleased to meet you, she said, holding out her hand. I hate that. People who come barging in. She explained that the door was open. That's why she'd come in. Shit. From the look of things, the crazy woman must come in anywhere she finds a hole.

I told her my aunt had died. That I was returning from the hospital. And that the burial would be the next day.

I took care of your aunt before she went into the hospital, Divani said. Bathed her. Cleaned the house. Rosa couldn't do anything anymore.

Afterwards, we stood there in silence, looking at that junk on the sofa. I stuck an aspirin in my mouth and felt the bitter taste.

Rosa was a big Corinthians fan, Divani said. Can I keep this key ring?

Before Divani left, I thought about asking her not to go around blabbing to her friends that I was in the area. But I don't like asking for favors. Owing anyone. People make demands. Even the good ones, the ones who say they took care of your aunt.

She must be new in the district, Divani. I didn't remember her, she wasn't from my time. As a matter of fact, there wasn't anyone from my time among the five who went to Aunt Rosa's funeral. I don't have any idea who the old couple was. And I hadn't seen the others either. I didn't recognize any of them.

If I hadn't wasted so much time with Eunice, in Nova Iguaçu, maybe Aunt Rosa would've still been alive when I got to São Paulo. You're not going to travel at night, Eunice said, when I called to find out about my aunt. Go tomorrow, early in the morning. That was Eunice's problem, too bossy. In the beginning she doubted everything I said. Once, she grabbed the phone out of my hand to check with the nurse how old Aunt Rosa was. I explained a million times that I was the only surviving family member, that after my cousin Robinson died Aunt Rosa became very sad.

You want me to start crying now or later? she asked.

Eunice had no heart.

At the cemetery, I regretted not coming earlier. Deep down, it was my fault. Too lazy to travel. I'll go next week, I thought, I'll go at Easter, I'll go for her birthday.

She died an hour ago, they told me when I got to the hospital.

What relation are you to her? the nurse asked.

Nephew.

I waited a long time till they led me to the room where they'd taken the body. We had to clear the room, someone explained. For another patient.

She spoke about you a lot, said the woman, as we walked down the corridors.

White as wax, hairless, a handful of skin and bone. This was all that was left of my family.

After the funeral, I walked in the sun down Avenida Rio Bonito to the bus stop.

It had been almost ten years since I'd been in São Paulo. Everyone building his own shack, I saw through the window of the bus. Brick, wood, tin, anything would do. Except paint. Everything gray. Traffic jammed. The same crap as always.

Don't go looking for a woman, said Eunice when she saw me to the door. You're coming back, aren't you?

I promised I would.

I liked her. The first time we fucked, she started saying how polite I was, I think you're cool because you're very polite. Later on, when I was living in her house, she told me she'd said that because of the size of my dick. A big dick, in my opinion, is gentlemanly. It's elegant. I'm going to get you a job with my brother, she'd said. But now I didn't know if I was going to go back. This wasn't Rio de Janeiro, it was Nova Iguaçu. It's all the same thing, Eunice said. But to me it wasn't. Rio was Rio. It blows your retinas away, like a song I once heard on the radio says. And Nova Iguaçu didn't blow anything away. It was a trap, that's what it was.

Máiquel, said a friend, we need a stand-up guy to pull a cool job, with heavy hitters. Heavy hitters, in this case, meant cops. The plan is simple, they explained. The cops stop the truck drivers and bring them to talk to us. A clean deal. The assholes just have to pay a toll, they cool their heels in a hideout while we take their ATM card, make withdrawals from nearby branches, and that's it. You'll be in charge of the hideout.

5

My job was to do nothing. To watch. From a distance. Not let the guys run off before the time. Right off the bat I saw there was nothing professional in the set-up. Working somebody over and breaking bones, that's what they liked. The day they killed a guy I got the hell out.

That was when I met Eunice. I went to buy chocolate and she was working at the checkout in the supermarket.

Hi, she said.

I didn't even think Eunice was all that pretty. But I didn't have anything to do, so I waited till her shift was over. That's how it began.

Later she told me her brother drove cargo all over Brazil. That he had a Scania 112 HW truck and lived in Mato Grosso, Goiás, Vitória, São Paulo, in high style. That was exactly what I wanted to do. Except I've got a problem. I'm a fugitive. I didn't mention that to Eunice, because I could take off on the highways along the Brazil-Bolivia border and who would find me?

My brother's going to introduce you to a good employment agent. He'll take care of all the documents for you.

False ones, I thought. If he can get legitimate ones, he can get fake ones. Eunice's brother was constantly traveling. Rondônia, Rio Grande do Sul. Meanwhile, my aunt was getting worse. And time was passing. What I was afraid of happened. And now there I was. Too late.

I got off the bus. There was no hurry, nothing to do. It was a pretty day, blue sky, air-quality unacceptable, said the sign on the avenue. Fewer trees, I noticed. More dogs. More noise. More dirt too. The square. Gonzaga's bar. I wondered if it still belonged to Gonzaga? I'd spent years thinking about that place. Believing it would be good to come back. Now, as I walked, I thought this stuff about places, to tell the truth, didn't make the slightest difference. Everywhere was the same, streets, houses, the city, I mean, what's the difference? It didn't change anything, me being there. The place, no matter where it is, doesn't bring peace of any kind. I'd had it.

I went back to the house, stretched out on the sofa, turned on the TV. It was strange to be in that living room, by myself. Everything empty. I mean, full. Of things, but without anything. Blender, broom, the sofa was new. I'm sending you some money, buy a new sofa. And she did buy one, Aunt Rosa.

On the bureau by the television, a photo of me and Cledir, at our wedding party. Cutting the cake. Bride and groom. And one of Robinson, at a barbecue, wearing flip-flops. Marcão. All of them dead. And another of Érica, with my daughter Samantha in her lap. I got up, picked up the picture frame, and went back to the sofa. So then, Érica, where did you disappear to, you child-kidnapper? Ten years. Ten years without seeing my daughter. Without news of Érica.

Suddenly, I felt something foul, a foul taste in my mouth. Hatred for that city, which only did bad things for me. I worked for them. I took care of those people. I did very important things. I even won a trophy. And my friends were dead. The house empty. Me there, a fugitive. Scumbags. Hatred for Érica especially. Érica shouldn't have done that to me. Running off with a preacher. Stealing my daughter. I'd been thinking about that a lot lately, going back, settling

7

everything once and for all. And every time I thought about it I felt more rage. Because it wasn't right, what she'd done. Stealing somebody else's daughter. What must Samantha be like? Eleven years and ten months, I thought. A young girl. What color would her hair be? I was alone now. Because of Érica. But I had a daughter. Who was mine. It was time to find Érica and my daughter. That's what I was going to do. I'd made up my mind.

2

I had a plan in mind but couldn't get started. That was my problem, beginning things. Getting off dead zero. I prefer not to make decisions. To let things ride. Sometimes I would turn on the radio and wander around the house with my hands in my pockets. I liked the place. Pots in the yard. Plastic flowers on the table. Papers. Rusty paperclips. Pennies. The image of the Virgin Mary, a souvenir of the day I was in Aparecida. Decals on the fridge. *Your Drugs Pharmacy. Best Prices. Fratelli Pizza.* Junk. What I liked most was having a house, a place of my own. I mean, not my own, but now it was. An inheritance. Kitchen, bedroom, living room. A neighborhood and a city. It had been a week since I'd been out. I would wake up, go to sleep, stay there, thinking stupid thoughts and eating crackers in front of the television.

I wanted to pay attention to the news, find out what was going on, but before I realized it I would be concentrating on the reporter, I mean on a piece of him, his large nose, his tiny mouth, his high forehead, his small teeth. And that way I never understood the news. Not at all. Only sometimes.

We're here in front of the Tatupé complex. The reporter's hair looked like a helmet. The wind was blowing but his hair didn't move, nothing. This local resident witnessed the escape of the adolescents from the Febem reformatory. How would you describe the scene?

It looked like that New Year's Eve marathon you see on television, replied the woman.

Good thing I wasn't there, I thought. I'm a fugitive.

What a dump, said Divani, looking around.

A strong black woman, Divani, muscular, with lots of cornrows. Now, because of the tight-fitting clothes, you could see her figure clearly. She hadn't even rung the doorbell but just barged in.

This place looks like a pigsty, she said, as I moved my sneakers out of her way. Just because your aunt died is no reason you have to be buried along with her.

I didn't want Divani to meddle in things, but she immediately started taking the dirty dishes to the sink, putting stuff away.

Do you know a detective in the area? I didn't want to involve Divani in my plans, I asked more than anything to get her to stop moving around, and two minutes later we were sitting in front of the computer, at her house, hunting for detectives.

Her mother, Dora, was there, as black as Divani, but faded and without her daughter's nice smile. Very white, Divani's teeth. So pretty they looked false.

But they're real, she assured me, the only thing fake here is this diamond, she said, showing me the ring on her finger. The two children watching television were hers. I'm a widow, she said. My husband got run over, two years ago. Bring him some coffee, Ma. Divani told me, as she turned on the computer, that she'd never forgiven her husband for dying like that. Smashed on the asphalt like mashed potatoes.

I drank the coffee, real sweet.

So stupid, my husband, continued Divani. It's one thing to die because it's your time. Cancer, that kind of thing. That's just fate. Getting run over is something else, completely different. It's what happens to poor stupid people. After Marcos died, I started noticing how people cross streets. The poor ones. Not me, 'cause I've got brains. They throw themselves under the cars. They don't even look. They've got nothing to lose, that's what I think. Living, dying, it's all the same. It must be a relief to die and not have bills to pay. It was Marcos who ran over the car, the driver himself told me that. The poor guy don't know how to cross a street.

Divani's breasts were the kind I like, the kind that fill your hands. She saw I was looking and it didn't bother her, she went on talking, all excited now, wigs, frozen foods, machines for making *churros*, shampoo, I've sold everything you could imagine, she said, but at the moment I'm unemployed. I don't work in telemarketing anymore, now I make a living teaching computer classes to people in the neighborhood. I have seven students.

Divani's hands were very pretty. Red nails. A fake diamond. I was dying for some pussy. But I didn't open my mouth. I didn't move. Friends' wives, virgins, women who are too pretty, and neighbors only if you're looking for trouble. I wanted peace.

Look at this, she said, after researching the Internet. There's no shortage of detectives. This one looks like he'd be good: *Put an End to Your Doubts*, the ad says.

I wrote down the address.

What do you want with a detective?

I want to find my daughter, I explained. She's eleven years old and she's disappeared.

Did she disappear with her mother?

No, her mother's dead, I said.

What a coincidence, she said. The two of us, widow and widower.

Now Divani seemed like some frisky young animal. People love meeting other people who're sinking in the same shit as them; that's the secret of Alcoholics Anonymous and all the anonymous-type crap in general. They don't go there to stop drinking, or stop fucking, or stop snorting but for the pleasure of seeing other people wallowing in the mud like them, or worse than them, if possible. Divani was there, looking at one more poor fuck; you're going to want to associate with me, I thought, the fucked-over widowers and neighbors.

It was a kind of kidnapping, I explained. Érica ran away and took my daughter with her.

Who's Érica?

My girlfriend, I answered.

Shit, some girlfriend, a real winner of a girlfriend, said Divani. How'd you ever get mixed up with that kind of people?

Dora said that she was leaving to take the kids to school.

I explained, when we were by ourselves, that I didn't like to talk about my life. Don't ask a lot of questions, I warned.

Before leaving I asked Divani not to mention anything to anybody.

Mention what?

All these things, I replied. About me. The fact that I'm here. I don't want anyone to know.

You're really weird, Máiquel. Really weird.

A barefoot little girl, looking at the camera I remember exactly the moment when I took that picture. Samantha, look at Daddy, look here, click. A pretty photo. A family. Samantha, Érica and me, a weekend in Ubatuba. We'd gone to the beach, I remember it clearly. We swam with Samantha in the hotel pool. We ate crab. We built a sandcastle on Tombo beach.

Saturday night Érica hired a babysitter to look after Samantha. I want to go to a nightclub, she said. I've had it up to here with bottles and dirty diapers.

I asked do you wanna dance, I hugged you, do you wanna dance, kissed you, one more dream doesn't make any difference, I even remember the song they were playing when Érica went out onto the floor, in a leather miniskirt, boots, bare shoulders.

What boots are those, Érica? It's too hot for boots.

So what? she said, I like them.

I punched a guy in the face who tried to mess with her in the nightclub. I don't remember how it played out. I was drunk. We ended up at the police station. Or maybe that was on another trip. I don't remember anymore. All I remember is that at the station Érica had to call my partner Santana, the bastard who ruined my life. It was because of him that everything fell apart, I know that now, it was his fault I lost Érica, Samantha, my friends, and everything good that I'd put together. Use up and throw away, that was his system. But not with me. Máiquel, I should've said before pulling the trigger and killing the traitor, Máiquel you don't throw away. Máiquel is here. And he's going to stay alive. Because Máiquel can take it. Máiquel is strong. Too bad you can't kill the same person twice. Maybe then I could stop thinking about those things, thinking about all that happened. Ten years have gone by, and I didn't choose to forget. I still remembered everything, every bit of it, feeling the urge to dig up the details.

Shit, man, Santana said that night, can't you drink without causing me such a hassle?

Funny how our heads work. All that stuff surfaced the moment I put the photo on the desk. That's her, I told the detective, that's my daughter.

Jonas seemed more interested in talking about spy cameras than in hearing my story. His office was a mess, a hole, with piles of paper and folders everywhere. I noticed that Jonas wore a toupee.

We're very reliable, he said. If it's a marital situation we only need a week to find out everything.

I have a hard time believing a guy who wears a rug.

If the guy's a detective, Jonas continued, and tells you two weeks, or a month, to solve the case, he's trying to rob you, that's my theory. Following a person, anybody can do that. What matters is our distinguishing characteristics. Spy cameras. Confidential reports. That's what matters. The only way I won't find your daughter is if she's dead, he promised.

I felt a chill run through my body.

He was slow to pay attention to the photo on his desk. He asked if it was the only one I had. I showed him another, of Samantha on Érica's lap. I said that Érica must be twenty-five. I spoke of Marlênio too, that son of a bitch preacher who took the two of them away, and his sect, Sacred Heart of Jesus or some such thing. I don't have a photo of him, I said. Jonas asked a bunch of questions and wrote my answers down on a pad. I spent nearly all afternoon in that stinking hole.

Before returning home I still had something I needed to do. My lawyer. It'd been a long time since me and him had spoken.

Tell him Máiquel is here, I said to the girl at the reception desk. Patrícia, her name was, there was an epidemic of Patrícias, I'd been noticing. Operators, clerks, sales ladies, it was like some kind of joke.

Two minutes later Mr Haroldo appeared. The living always turn up, he said. Come on in, we'll have some coffee.

I could see he wasn't at all happy. Mr Haroldo was one of my lawyers in the days when I made money killing people. A friend of my partners. Also a son of a bitch. He didn't have a paunch anymore or a mustache. Scumbags have changed their appearance. Nowadays they're slim. They do liposuction to get rid of their bellies. They're all the time dieting, the fuckers.

15

You're a real phenomenon, boy, he said when the coffee came. What hole have you been hiding in?

Brazil, I said. An enormous hole.

I almost didn't recognize you with black hair, he said. I was used, you know, to that rocker style of yours. Idle talk. He was afraid of me, Mr Haroldo.

I explained that I wanted to sell my aunt's house. I'm the sole heir, I said. I felt like laughing at that word, heir. Poor Aunt Rosa. That fucked-up house.

That's easy, he replied, you just have to give me power of attorney, that's all.

No one knows I'm here, I said.

Nor will they, Mr Haroldo answered. A lawyer is like a priest. What happens here is a professional secret.

That's good, I said, it'd be shit if the police found me right after I come to see you.

The newly thin man got the message. I'll send my people this very day to see about it for you. Rest easy.

Great. Then I gave him the information about a savings account of Aunt Rosa's. I want to close this account, I said. Take out all the money.

On the way home I passed by Gonzaga's bar, which now had a neon sign advertising lunch. Was that Gonzaga, the toad-faced guy with the beer belly, behind the counter? Strange how men in their old age start looking like their mothers. I never met Gonzaga's mother, but he was her spitting image. A female toad. Perfect. I felt like going in but then thought I'd better not.

When I got home, everything was different. The living room was clean, the floor waxed, the bathroom scrubbed.

Clothes were hanging on the line. Divani's work. A note was on the kitchen table. *Some stressed-out woman named Eunice phoned. I told her to take a walk.* Jeez. Eunice must've been mad as hell. *And I made an orange cake, it's in the oven. Very good, the cake.*

How did Divani manage to get into the house? Through the broken window, it had to be that. And I'm the weird one. Women are crazy.

3

Names of every kind, *Jesus Here and You with Him*, *Trumpet of God*, I was reading the list of evangelical churches that Jonas the detective brought me. *Daisies of Jesus*, *God's Winds*, sounds like a fart, I said, God's wind is a fart. *City of the Lambs of God*, you want me to read all this? I asked. Three pages of nothing but the names of evangelical churches.

Jonas said that without the name of the church it was going to be hard to locate my daughter and Érica. Assuming they're still in that guy Marlênio's church, he added. I only listed those that have Jesus or God in their names, because you told me Marlênio's church was Jesus-Something-or-Other. There's lots of others. You know? They're impressive, these evangelicals, Jonas continued, a little awkward.

All that talk in his office the week before, I-just-need-seven-days-to-solve-your-case, was pure bullshit, and that was very clear to both of us. Jonas was eating on my money, and he wouldn't stop talking or pacing up and down. I don't like that, agitation, it makes me nervous.

I went to get information from one of the parishioners, said Jonas, and gave up. The guy immediately tried to convince me that the camel was proof of the existence of God. If that's true, then why don't people in the backlands have a hump too? The idea's my own, Jonas added. People in the backlands undergo just as much privation as camels. If God provided for the camel and forgot the people in the backlands, then God doesn't exist. People in the backlands are fucked. That's the proof God doesn't exist. If God did exist, backlands people would have to have a hump and drink a hundred liters of water in ten minutes too, to put up with the drought and the hunger. They don't take that into consideration.

It seemed like Jonas was never going to shut up, and I had a lot of things to do. Is this all you've got for me? I asked. A week's work and this is the result?

That's not a report, Jonas replied. Your case is atypical. We're completely in the dark. I work from the material the client brings me. What do you know about your daughter? Nothing, he answered his own question. An obnoxious type, I noted. You went ten years without any contact at all, he continued. His face was pockmarked. A guy who used to have the mange. You don't even have a recent photo, he said. You know nothing about the girl who ran off with her, or the church that took them in. I can't do miracles. That's for their Lord, for Érica's husband, I just work on the basis of clues.

And he left, in his ridiculous hairpiece, but not without first promising to have news soon.

I didn't want to waste any more time. That same afternoon, I went to a used-car lot. You're in luck, this is a cream puff, said the salesman, as I drove around the block in a navy-blue '93 Volks. I liked the color, discreet. Reasonable mileage. It had been a long time since I'd been behind the wheel. The previous owner was a doddering old man, continued the salesman when we arrived back at the lot, explaining that the car almost never left the garage. Roomy trunk. Powerful Heart of Jesus.

And, there, parking the Volks, I finally remembered the name of Marlênio's church. Can I use your phone? I asked the salesman. I called Jonas. I'm sure of it, I said, you can look for it, that's the name of the sect.

This makes the job easier, he said, a whole lot easier.

The salesman was with another salesman, on the sidewalk, smoking. A real bargain, he said when he saw me again. We have a waiting list of people interested in cars like this.

I paid cash and left there driving my Volks, happy that I had enough money left over for what I needed to do.

I didn't think Aunt Rosa had a lot in the bank. Nine thousand and thirty *reais*, was what Mr Haroldo told me the day before when he called me to hand it over.

The truth is, Aunt Rosa had spent hardly anything of what I sent her all that time. A dumb life, that. Something I've never been able to believe in is the future, making plans, economizing, savings, all that crazy stuff. I spend everything I get, as fast as I can. That's the way life is. Waiting in line for death. People dying every day, run over, from cancer, getting shot in the face. You wait in line, without knowing, and then your number comes up. That's what I believe. In the line. I also believe that I could be recognized out in the street, at any time. Hey, aren't you Máiquel, the hired killer? The one who's better than barbed wire? Better than trenches? Better than armored doors? The one who killed Santana? The one who riddled with bullets the belly of Dr Carvalho, that son of a bitch of a dentist? No one remembered about the Man of the Year anymore. For services to the community. Or the scum I took off the streets, everybody had forgot that. Now and then people remembered me, but it was always in some account about dangerous killers. Wanted, they said. One of the most wanted. I wouldn't go back to prison, that I'd decided. In a cell breathing the same air as twenty, thirty, a horde of lowlifes, never. No fucking way I'd ever be a prisoner. I'd rather die.

From the car lot I went straight to Two Brothers, who really were brothers, document counterfeiters in São Bernardo. I had once done some work for them, just one job actually; I killed, we killed, me and my team, a kid they called Russo, who had held up their office eight times. Russo's rap sheet was impressive, he would telephone the places before he robbed them and ask, How much you got in the till? Depending on the answer he would change the day for taking action. It's too little, he'd say, get some more together and wait for me, because if I go there and there's no money, somebody's gonna pay the price. And if you call the police, you'll really get fucked, he warned. Russo was a minor, he was constantly being arrested and let go. On one occasion he raped a secretary. We were very efficient. A single bullet in the middle of the forehead. Everybody loved it.

Now, one of the brothers looked at me with a blank expression, as if he didn't know me. He wasn't sure how to act. He thought I was dead, or in jail, and suddenly I show up, now what? You still into that business? Counterfeiting crap? Nowadays everything's different, he said.

I'll pay whatever's necessary, I answered. I want a fake ID and a driver's license.

Things were just the same as always. All you had to do was pay. Nothing changes, in reality, if you have money and are willing to pay the price. And I was. I couldn't head out unprepared.

That night I called Divani to have a pizza. She wanted to go by car, Let's take the kids, they love riding in cars. Divani was happy, we invited her mother to come along.

Going out was a mistake, I saw right away. You have to think about the worst if you're a fugitive. At the pizzeria, for example. You have to think that they, the scumbags, are going to come in, recognize you, and call the police. That's the way you avoid problems. So you don't even go into the pizzeria. You don't even go out of the house in certain situations, you stay put, away from the noise, the confusion. I lost my appetite. I put some money on the table and told Divani I'd wait for her in the car.

She didn't understand anything, but I didn't care. I thought it best not to take any chances. I turned on the radio and listened to an interview. Nowadays they don't want you to say things look black, that's prejudiced, said the politician, or say midget, fairy, welfare queen; they call the rich corrupt, said the speaker, and the poor thieves. That's true, you have to call everybody a thief, I thought. There was a government primer that condemned it. It also condemned dyke and fag. I liked that.

Soon, Divani appeared with the children. What happened, Míquel?

I've got a headache, I said.

We returned home in silence.

Ciao, said Divani, getting out at her house. Are you going to sleep now?

I said I was.

Divani was cool, but I had other plans. I got into bed and tossed and turned. Suddenly, I felt a crazy urgency to change my life, to find Érica, to have my daughter close to me, maybe it was still possible to do something, I thought, the three of us together again, start over somewhere, Brazil is so large, nobody knows who you are if you don't want them to, if Érica could forgive me, if I can forgive Érica, together, with phony papers, whatever, we could start a new life in some small town, a job, all of that ran through my head. I went to the living room to look for the photograph of them. Érica in shorts, slim, short hair. I liked Érica so much, and I was so enraged when she went away. Why complicate things? No, it was just a matter of going after her, I thought, forgetting, resolving everything, putting things right, I'm Samantha's father, for shit's sake, she's got my daughter, for shit's sake. I went back to the bedroom, stretched out on the bed, and looked at the photos. Érica had to understand the situation. I closed my eyes and thought, thought, almost managing to recall what that time was like, the sounds of our house, words like 'syrup' and 'clowns', which for a long time I avoided saying. They reminded me of Érica, which would make me roll on the floor in pain; now I still went on suffering but it was different, I wanted to look for them, wanted to find my daughter, wanted to tell Érica that I knew by heart every word in the damned note she wrote the day she went away and that it stayed in my pocket for a long time. I carried it with me for years. *Máiquel, I still love you, but I swear to you I'm going to find somebody really great to love. And I'm going to be a very happy girl, you'll see. As for you, I hope you get fucked, that's what I hope. I want your life to turn to shit, a living hell, and for you never to be able to forget me, and that every woman in your life is stupid, that's what you deserve, you imbecile.* Signed, *Érica.* Did Samantha know I was her father?

Don't you lock your door? asked Divani, coming into the bedroom. She sat on the bed, beside me. I came to see if you're any better.

I'm fine, I said.

What's that? she asked, pointing to a piece of the tattoo on my right arm. An F. Some woman's name, I bet. I showed her the rest, raising the sleeve of my T-shirt. *Fuck you*, was what was written. You're weird, she said. Divani smelled good, of soap, lime. Know why I came here? she asked. She stretched out on the bed and kissed me. Turn out the light, she said. I'm ashamed of my body.

That was just silly. Divani's body was to die for.

★　　★　　★

I woke up around noon with the telephone ringing. It was a girl who worked for Two Brothers, to say that my documents were ready. All I had to do was stop by and pick them up.

I took a shower and went out to get something to eat. I picked up the documents. Rogério da Silva Pereira was my new name. I liked it. Rogério. A rich man's name. Or a poor man's, it made no difference. These days the poor have rich people's names and vice versa.

As I was leaving, one of the brothers came running after me. Máiquel, he said, can I offer you some coffee?

We went to the corner bar. I showed him the documents.

We're good at that, he said proudly, they came out great, I'd already seen them. After some beating around the bush, he asked if I still had a set-up.

What kind of set-up? I asked the question just to see the guy stammer.

You used to know how to put an end to people, he said.

I unlearned, I said. My specialty now is avoiding the police.

There's a guy, he said, with a job.

I'm out, I said.

Too bad, they pay well, don't you know somebody? he asked.

I can check, how much do they pay?

Actually, he answered, it would have to be you, it involves trustworthy people.

I felt like laughing. You want to kill your wife? I asked.

My brother, he replied right to my face. I'll pay a hundred grand. Fifty now, fifty after the job. It's complicated, you know? Me and his wife, we're having an affair, he said, the

25

bald-faced bastard, with a little smile, as if I understood the dirty dealing.

I know, I said. But I don't kill cuckolds or work for queers. You'll have to find somebody else.

I spent the rest of the day wandering the streets with that rattling in my head. Before going home, I stopped at a pay phone. I thought about calling and warning the cuckold. Watch out for your wife. And your brother. Fuck it, I thought. What did I have to do with those scumbags?

When I got home, an employee of Mr Haroldo's was showing the house to an interested party.

Divani was there too, pouting. The house has a lot of problems, she did me the favor of saying. Leaks. The street is noisy. Could you tell me what's going on? she asked, pulling me aside. Why are you selling the house? When I answered that I wanted to look for my daughter, Divani lost her cool, saying I didn't need to do that, looking for missing people is the job of the police. You can stay here, Máiquel, she said, you can find a job.

After the prospective buyer left, she pulled me onto the sofa. Sit here. Do you like me? she asked.

Yes.

How much?

You're really cool, I said.

Of course I'm cool. I know that. What I asked is how much you like me. I want to know if you're able to do something different from what you were thinking of doing, Máiquel. Whether we can talk. How much do you like me?

26

Just then the phone rang. It was Eunice. When are you coming back? she asked. My brother's here. I spoke to him about you and he said he can arrange a job for you.

I bought a car, I replied. A Volkswagen. Blue. You'll love it.

I don't know what came over Divani. She was like an animal, she grabbed the phone from my hand and threw it out the window. And then she left, cursing me.

Are you crazy, Divani? How am I supposed to talk on the phone now?

Divani must have really been pissed at me, because she didn't show up the next day, or the day after that.

Mr Haroldo sent two more buyers, one of them interested enough to come back twice, once with his wife, once with his whole family.

We're going to close the deal this week, Mr Haroldo's employee promised me.

Friday night I was tired of doing nothing. I called Jonas.

I don't like giving out information in small chunks, he said. You'll be getting a complete report soon.

Afterwards, I put on my sneakers and went to Divani's house.

She didn't even say hi and went on staring at the computer screen. I played with the kids, watched TV and ate some of Dora's beans.

I miss you, I said shortly before leaving.

Go chase yourself, she replied.

It was almost ten at night when the doorbell rang. I opened it.

Hi, said Divani.

She came in, and with her was a man with a shaven head, a husky mulatto. How's it going?

This is Bruno, she said, he's a police corporal and knows a lot of people, I told him about your daughter, and I think he can help.

4

It felt like I was falling from someplace high. But I was there, standing like an idiot, dizzy, not understanding why Divani had brought a cop into my home. He knows someone who works in Anti-Kidnapping, she said.

It wasn't a kidnapping, I said.

You said it was a kidnapping. If they run off with your daughter without permission it's kidnapping.

But I don't want the police involved, I said, it's my family, my wife.

Divani clicked her tongue. Now this. You said Érica is your ex-girlfriend, Máiquel, an ex-girlfriend isn't a wife. Your wife died, aren't you a widower? Divani asked, irritated.

Bruno was looking at me with a funny expression, I didn't like it. Did he recognize me? I felt like smacking Divani.

Well, I'm just here to help, I can wait outside, the policeman said.

Stay here, Bruno, don't go away, I don't understand Máiquel. A few days ago he was looking for a detective, and now he refuses the help of the police? Máiquel, Bruno was nice enough to come here after I told him about your case. Her hands on her hips, a shrill voice. Divani, I saw at that moment, could get awful nasty. A snoop. He told me, Máiquel, that everybody who tries to solve a kidnapping on his own ends up regretting it.

Divani, I explained, it's not a kidnapping, you don't know the details.

Ah, well, Divani sighed, there's the details, they must be real tough, the details, they run off with your daughter and you don't even call the police, what kind of details can they be?

The cop and Divani stared at me, waiting for an answer.

At that moment the doorbell rang again. I ran to open the door, dying to get out of that situation. If Muhammad won't go to the mountain, Eunice said, the mountain will go to Muhammad. Eunice, in sneakers and her hair in a ponytail, carrying a backpack, came in without ceremony. Hi, folks, I'm Máiquel's girlfriend, she said. Is everything okay, sweetie? Cool, your aunt's house, I hope you've got something to eat, I'm starving. I'm going to take a bath, go ahead with your conversation.

Divani skewered me with her eyes. Bruno, she said, let's go. I don't know why I wasted my time with this idiot.

As soon as they left I ran to the bathroom. Eunice was in the shower. She leaned out to give me a kiss, stuck her tongue in my mouth. Did you like the surprise?

Why didn't you let me know you were coming? I asked, looking out the window to make sure the cop and Divani weren't around any longer.

I've been calling you for five days, she answered. Your phone must be broken. Who were those two? Are you worried about something?

We're getting out of here today, I said.

Why? I like this house. Can't we stay here a few days? Eunice was on vacation from the supermarket and her idea was 'to stay a month.' They tell me São Bernardo has a really cool shopping mall.

While Eunice finished her bath, I packed my bag.

Then I put our things in the car, turned out the lights, locked the house, and we got the hell out of there.

Shakespeare in Love, can I buy the poster? Eunice asked. I just love posters. The problem with taking Eunice downtown was that she wanted to buy everything she saw. And I'm going to take this one, *Miss Congeniality*, for my co-worker. She loves posters too.

We were staying at the Hotel Los Angeles, on Aurora, and every morning Eunice would drag me out to look at stuff, even auto-parts stores, in Duque de Caxias, that she wanted to go into. So I can tell my brother about it, I might come across something interesting, a different kind of horn, cheap, and later, I don't know, in Rio de Janeiro they don't have those new things, at least I've never seen them. They say that here in São Paulo everything's cheaper.

We went to Sete de Abril, in the Dom José de Barros district and environs, and saw those stores of precious and semiprecious stones, full of gringos and tourists, walked along Consolação, and Eunice made me buy a lamp for her house. Then we went to the Pagé Gallery; I'd never in my life seen so much junk.

This is wonderful, she said. Toys, linens, costume jewelry, she wanted to see and touch everything, ask the price. Look here, Máiquel, cutlery, let's go over there. She didn't even know what cutlery was. But she wanted to see it. I feel like shouting when I see this pile of things to buy. I could spend five thousand in a couple of hours, she said. I'm a world-class shopper. I'm a real buyer. I love buying things. I should've been born an American. They say that Americans are born buying. For me there's nothing in the world better than buying. If I'm feeling a bit down, all I have to do is buy a new blouse, or earrings, and the sadness goes away. This is the life I was born for.

When on rua São Caetano Eunice discovered stores that sold wedding gowns, she went crazy. She wanted to go into every one of them.

What, are you by any chance getting married? I asked.

Of course I am. To you, she said. I'm going to choose my dress now, to speed things up. And our son is going to have a nice name, because Eunice is horrible. Eunice sounds awful. Eu-nuch. Use-less. Look over there, Máiquel, wholesale and retail, let's go in. I love wholesale and retail.

The price of things in Crackland turned Eunice into a spectacle for the street vendors. Máiquel, look at this, buy one sandwich and get three juices. Three juices, she shouted. I'm dying of thirst. A pair of shoes for six *reais*.

I had to ask her to calm down. People were turning their heads to look at Eunice laughing like crazy in the street.

The hotel was full of prostitutes and drug dealers. There's no better way in the world to make money than sex and drugs, and that's the truth.

At night we would eat in some restaurant around Praça da República and take in the scene, whores, pimps, trash. Everything bad, they had it there.

The owner of our hotel told me to watch out for gangs of drug dealers. The greatest danger, according to him, was on rua Guaianazes, which was run by Nigerians. Don't go near there. Those blacks only speak their own language, and they'll stick a knife in you before you can count to three.

Later I found out that he was a dealer too and was part of another gang, enemy of the Africans.

The good thing about São Paulo is that here you've got everything, the guy said, you got gay movie theaters, drag theaters, theaters for people who only like blow jobs. You can find anything in this city. Everything. You just have to look. Next door is a guy who sells nothing but thimbles. Of all kinds. Even made from recycled paper. That's why I love this city. I don't think I'll ever need a thimble, but it gives me real peace of mind to know that, if I do, there's a thimble store right here, understand? Think about Carnival. Where do you think the samba schools in Rio buy their feathers, spangles, sequins and all the fancy get-ups they wear in the parades? Here. In São Paulo. Without São Paulo the Rio Carnival would be nothing. That's what São Paulo is. Possibilities. Offers.

I spent the days wandering around, looking at store windows with Eunice.

All this is very odd, she said. An ugly land, lots of people, lots of poverty, lots of money, lots of buildings, lots of whores, lots of trash, lots of traffic, I think I prefer Rio.

As if it was any different.

It *is* different, she said. Here all that's missing is a fence, with the rich on one side and the poor on the other.

Jonas and my lawyer knew where I was staying. Now there was nothing to do but wait.

Wednesday night Haroldo called to say that Aunt Rosa's house was practically sold. He also said that, the day he took the buyer to see the house, Divani showed up and handed him a letter to give to me.

Give it to me later, I said.

She got hold of my phone number, Haroldo continued, and calls me every day, five or six times, to find out if you got the letter. The woman is desperate.

Don't worry about it, I said.

One last question: the buyer wants the house empty, what do I do with the stuff in it?

Go see Divani, I answered, and offer it to her. Whatever she doesn't want, throw it out.

What did Divani have to tell me? I didn't like Haroldo's attitude. Intimacy. There are guys who, just because they've known you for ten years, think they're your friend.

The next day, I woke up to Jonas telling me to come to his office. You're going to like what I have for you.

★　　★　　★

34

They're in Campo Grande, Jonas said as soon as I sat down in the armchair across from his desk. Mato Grosso do Sul.

I opened the brown envelope that he handed me.

You didn't tell me that woman is rich, commented Jonas, when I started looking at the photos.

Érica was all made-up, her hair tied back, getting out of a large car in front of a fancy restaurant. I felt my heart beating faster.

They've been living there for three years, you know how it is, evangelicals are in seventh heaven in Mato Grosso, there's lots of whores there, lots of drugs and lots of Arabs, it's a field day for them.

Érica was pretty. But what floored me was my daughter, in uniform, standing at the school entrance with girlfriends.

Samantha is this one, Jonas said.

He didn't need to say anything. She was the mirror image of Cledir. It took my breath away.

There are more, said Jonas.

Érica and Samantha crossing the street, holding hands. Érica opening the car door for Samantha to get in. Érica and Samantha coming out of the house, in gym clothes and with a dog on a leash. The two of them arriving at church. Marlênio, the prick, wasn't in any of them.

Yes he is, said Jonas, here he is, the one in the suit.

I hadn't recognized him. He was whiter. He looked like a leading man, Marlênio. All cool, in dark glasses, coat and tie.

They're married, Jonas said. And your daughter has his last name.

At that moment I saw I was wasting my time. What sense was there in going after Samantha? What could I say to her?

They've got a very good life, Jonas continued. The Church is sucking in more and more fools. Just look at the house where they live, it's even got a swimming pool. Érica is a bishop, and it appears her worship services are a success. Actually, she's the one who runs the church. Her husband travels a lot. Look at her in a suit, in the pulpit, giving the Devil hell. Look at them at their country place, near Campo Grande. Take a look.

More photos, Érica in a bikini, holding a cellphone. A great body, firm. You can bet she's got a lover, I thought. At least that was Érica's theory. Fitness centers make their money from adulteresses, she used to say. It's cheating women who like fitness centers. The ones who claim they like working out are barefaced liars. That's what Érica used to say. And now she had a well-toned body, firm all over. Red toenails. Samantha and her friends swimming.

It's what I always say, those Bible-thumpers forbid pleasure only to others. They themselves really live it up. Here's the address, the phone number, everything's here. The address of the girl's school. And on this piece of paper, Jonas said, showing me a sheet, you've got your daughter's schedule.

Daily
    7.15: Samantha leaves for school
    12.30: Érica, Marlênio, or the maid picks up Samantha from school. Address: 12 rua das Américas

Monday

   3.00: Private computer class, at home, with the teacher
   from the church
Tuesdays and Thursdays
   4.00–5.15: Violin lesson at the church
   Address: 432 rua Visconde de Albuquerque
Wednesdays and Fridays
   2.00–3.30: English lesson at American World
   Address: 36 Avenida Lagoinha
Friday evening
   7.00: Choir practice at the church

Jonas also gave me videotapes showing Érica and Marlênio preaching. She's really good, he said; when she starts talking about the Antichrist, about hunger, about Hell, the pale horse, it's frightening.

I left with the reports, the photos, all the material.

P.S. One more thing, you idiot. I never went to bed with Marlênio and never will. That was in the note Érica had written me when she ran away with Marlênio. I memorized that too. No need to, it was a lie. Marlênio was her husband. And the father of my daughter. So many assholes she could marry and she had to go and choose that loser. Goddammit.

I opened the bag, the money was there, eighteen grand.

I've already taken out my commission, Haroldo said. The house sold for a nice price. A good deal.

We were in my room at the Hotel Los Angeles. Eunice

37

had gone for a walk, my idea. Can I buy some little things? she'd asked. Little things, magic words to Eunice.

Sure, buy anything you like. Be back in time for lunch.

Haroldo left and I opened Divani's letter. *Máiquel, please forgive me for that day. I like you. A lot. A whole lot. Máiquel, I know you got annoyed because of Bruno, but, you know, I was just trying to help. Bruno knows a lot of people there in the police, but if you'd rather look for your daughter on your own, I understand. But don't leave without saying goodbye to me, I think at least we could be friends. A kiss from your Divani.*

Poor Divani, I felt sorry for her.

I waited until lunchtime, and Eunice appeared, loaded down with shopping bags.

We left to go eat. At the restaurant, I explained that I was going after my daughter in Mato Grosso and it would be better for her to return to Nova Iguaçu.

I'll go with you, she said. I always wanted to see Mato Grosso, and anyway I'm on vacation. From there we can go back to Nova Iguaçu.

I don't know if I'll be going back to Nova Iguaçu, I explained.

Yes you are, I'll persuade you.

It's a long way, I said, things could get complicated.

I know, said Eunice, you don't want that woman, that stuck-up woman who stole your daughter, to meet your current wife. I saw the photos of that bitch, yesterday, while you were asleep. She's a criminal and ought to be arrested. I'll beat her to a pulp if she doesn't let you speak to Samantha.

38

She loves Samantha, I explained.

And you still defend that kidnapper?

Eunice packed our bags while I went to get the car, which was in a parking garage nearby.

On the way, I had the impression I was being followed.

It was 3.15 when I entered the building. I went up the stairs to the fourth level, where my car was. The place stank to high heaven.

As I was opening the car door, I saw behind me the cop, Bruno. Hi there, Máiquel, what a coincidence, he said.

Coincidence my ass, I said.

That night, at your house, I didn't recognize you. It wasn't till later that I remembered you, man. The great Máiquel. You killed a lot of people, didn't you, bro?

I felt a tremendous urge to beat the shit out of the guy.

You know, he continued, those were good times. Nowadays we can't even slap around a minor without it becoming a federal case.

Spit it out, I said, say what you got to say, I'm in a hurry.

I called Divani, Bruno said, and told her, Divani, Máiquel is the biggest killer in São Paulo.

Now Bruno was looking at me in a funny way. It was Divani who gave me the address of your lawyer, he continued. After that, it was simple. All I had to do was follow the trail.

What do you want? I asked.

There's a warrant out on you, one I unfortunately have to carry out, you know? You're under arrest, he said.

I started laughing. Son of a bitch. Another fucker in my life. Dude, how much do you want? I asked.

Remember Neno? he said. That child you killed? Neno was my cousin.

Shit. I did remember. Remembered everything. The hatred I felt. I knocked on the door, Neno, the kid they hired me to kill, appeared. He appeared and didn't give me time to do anything. He jumped over walls, jumped over fences, turning right and left, with me behind him. Neno ran into a bar, crouched behind the counter. Everybody on the floor, I said. I approached, ready to fire, Neno was kneeling beside the Coca-Cola bottles, praying. He asked me for the love of God not to kill him. But I didn't believe in God anymore. I believed in ulcers. I'm going to kill you, you son of a bitch, because starting today I'm the killer. I'm the bars on the window, the watchdog, the wall, the broken glass. I'm the killer. Bang, bang, bang.

I remembered everything.

It took me a long time to place you, man, because of that ratty hair of yours, which used to be blond and is black now, Bruno said. It was because of my cousin that I became a cop. Because of Neno. I swore I'd catch sons of bitches like you and put them in prison.

And now, he said, but I interrupted, pop, pop, pop, I put three bullets in his head.

My weapon was inside my jacket. I'd been going around armed for days. For security. He should've thought of that. These guys are a bunch of wimps.

I left his body where it fell, there in the garage.

I started the car and got out of there, fast.

5

The highway's a good place for thinking. You put the car in fifth gear and thoughts come out of nowhere, from some black hole, you see an ad for life insurance for the entire family, a family at the dinner table, smiling, Daddy, Mommy, and the kids, and you think about that being the best time to strike, when everybody is stuffing themselves, and then the thoughts continue, one after the other. And before you know it you're thinking things, bang, the day I die, worms, rot, the end, no one lives here anymore, just an empty shell, this car will become a piece of junk, scrap, everybody starts dying off, the ones you know, almost nobody is left, and you go on with your thoughts, stirring around back there, raging, loving, hating, forgetting, and the thing keeps growing, or it doesn't, because Eunice interferes a lot, with her habit of reading road signs out loud and talking endlessly.

Since I was a little girl, you know, Máiquel? When I learned to read I saw there was no turning back. I would go out with my mother and read anything I saw, prices, banners, lists, license plates, posters, ads, everything. My mother was illiterate and wanted me to read some piece of information for her, bus routes, that kind of thing, so I felt the need to read anything I saw. It was an awful feeling, the way the letters would attack me, and sometimes I'd have to close my eyes just to get some rest. I'm still that way today. I mean, I don't close my eyes, I read everything. But I don't suffer. If it's written down, I read it.

But can't you read quietly? I asked.

No, she couldn't, she had to read aloud. Because she was used to it. Look at that one. This lot for sale and others even better. Gee, Máiquel, who's going to buy this one if they sell others that are better? And if you think Nova Iguaçu is ugly, what about Osasco? It's polluted, trash everywhere.

Shit, I couldn't even think.

But then I thought, when Eunice left me in peace for a moment, Érica is married to Marlênio. I've done a lot of bad things in my life, and one of them was not killing that preacher. I hit him in the mouth, a long time ago, he fell down, and when he got up, with cut lips, punch, he said that if I confessed to killing my wife Cledir to the police, punch, if we felt remorse for our shortcomings, punch, and our sins, punch, we would be saved, punch, and escape the fires of Hell. I hit him in the face again, and even on the ground he went on vomiting Bible verses, saying that God didn't intend us for wrath, I didn't let him finish the sentence, I climbed on top of him. God is slow to anger, he said, and I beat on him until my arms ached.

I've already got God's forgiveness, Marlênio. And if God feels I still owe anything, I'll come back and kill you. Why didn't I finish the job?

Can you stop so I can pee, love?

We had just left Osasco. Industrial District of Votupoca, Barueri, sheesh, what ugly names, Eunice said, reading the signs.

We stopped at a gas station, I went to get a soda.

When she returned from the restroom, I asked if she wanted anything.

Chewing gum, she said, for the trip. And water. Chocolate candy. Things for when hunger hits you.

We bought everything and went back to the car.

Is it far to Campo Grande? Eunice asked.

If you get tired, I can put you on a bus for home, I answered.

Eunice made herself comfortable, leaned against the window, took off her shoes and put her feet in my lap. Give up? she said. I'm with you to the end. My vacation is just beginning. Oh, it's great not having anything to do. I love it. Why haven't you gone after your daughter before now?

If you're going to stay with me, I replied, it's better not to ask so many questions.

You've got no trespass written all over you, she said. Don't do this, don't do that. What else don't I know about you?

Lots of things, I admitted, I'm a dangerous killer. A fugitive. I've blown away lots of people.

She didn't know whether to believe me. She laughed nervously. Good thing you're a great fuck, she said. She stuck a piece of gum in my mouth. I'd like to know more about that woman, that Érica. Did the two of you fuck often? Eunice was trying to turn me on, sticking her foot between my legs. I already had a hard-on.

Want to fuck? I asked.

You animal, she said.

You bitch, I replied. Whore, fox.

You savage, she said.

We always played around like that.

I love eating your pussy.

Go on talking, she said. Don't you want to stop the car?

I looked in the rearview mirror but didn't find a safe place.

Máiquel, Eunice shouted, look out.

I tried to brake but there wasn't time. I heard the thud of the collision.

We killed him, Eunice said when I stopped the car.

Three legs, shit. If he had four, I told Eunice, there'd be time, he wouldn't die, but three? Actually, he had four, but only three worked, the fourth was a kind of second tail. That's what I noticed when I put the animal in the car. My heart was broken. He was a large mongrel who was nothing but skin and bones, hairy, ready to die.

If he survived, he would just be a problem, Eunice said to

console me. A crippled dog is a horrible thing. Worse than people. People can at least use a wheelchair.

I was feeling rotten, but he was still breathing when we got to the clinic in Araçariguama. I'm going to ask for a rag to clean the trunk, I said. We'd been waiting over half an hour for news. Once the blood dried, it would be hard to clean.

The receptionist gave me a rag and some alcohol, and as I was leaving, Eunice called me. The vet, she said, pointing to a nice-looking woman in a white smock.

Your dog is all right, she said, smiling, he just needed some stitches in the head. Want to see him?

Shit-colored, all fucked-up, pretty women like that, blonde, who take good care of themselves, made me feel like the dog on the stretcher. Goddamn, they'd shaved his head to put in the stitches and the poor devil looked even uglier. He gazed at me in fear, frightened and weak.

Eunice made a point of emphasizing that the animal wasn't ours. We ran over him, she said more than once.

Do you plan to keep him? the veterinarian asked.

Isn't he going to die? asked Eunice, disappointed.

I didn't like Eunice's attitude. The only thing missing was for her to ask the woman to kill the dog. That thing crossed the road, she said. We didn't see it. We're not responsible. It could happen to anybody.

I felt enraged at Eunice. Shit. I'm taking him with us, I answered.

Eunice frowned. And she went on sighing and complaining while the vet explained that the dog was dehydrated, undernourished, and that the best thing would be for him to stay in the clinic on fluids for two days.

Two days here, with nothing to do, in this shithole of a town? Eunice asked, back in the car, while I drove around in search of a hotel. And we're even going to take that animal with us?

It wasn't easy finding a place.

It's the Artichoke Festival, flowers and wine, the city's jammed, said the young woman at the reception desk who took us to the room.

Eunice's mood had improved. Hear that, Máiquel? Isn't that cool, the Artichoke Festival?

We showered and went downstairs for dinner. We're on the São Roque side, said Eunice, looking at a pamphlet on the table. There's a day trip through the Atlantic Forest, you can see the waterfalls. Why don't we do it?

You can go if you want to, I said. I'm going to stay with Tiger.

Tiger?

My dog, I explained.

Are you by any chance interested in that stuck-up woman at the clinic? Eunice asked.

I'm interested in my dog, I replied.

That mutt isn't even yours, Máiquel.

Get used to it, I said.

Eunice pouted through the rest of dinner. She said she wasn't about to take care of any dog, that he stank, he had fleas, and that it was crazy for me to take him with us on 'our vacation' just because of 'the accident.'

46

There is no 'our vacation,' I said. I'm looking for my daughter, and you can leave now if you want.

You're selfish, she said. A womanizer. I know very well what you're interested in. I saw how you looked at that woman.

We went back to the hotel, I took out one of the tapes that Jonas had given me and left Eunice there, scowling, Turn out the light, she said when I left.

I asked at the reception desk if there was a videotape player I could use.

Only my father's, said the girl, pointing to a man in Bermudas and slippers at the hotel entrance.

A stupid situation. Me, in the living room of the house next door, watching Érica preach.

We're evangelicals ourselves, said the man. Make yourself comfortable. Hallelujah, brother, may the peace of the Lord be with you. The dog, his wife, everybody there. The smell of steak cooking in the kitchen. Would you like something to eat?

No thanks, I said. I take pleasure in suffering, Érica was preaching. In pain. What a pile of crap. Érica was loaded with dough, raking it in from suckers and talking about need.

For when I am weak, then I am strong. II Corinthians 12:10, and it is on that, brethren, that we will reflect today.

Sometimes I broke out laughing.

Whoever comes to my church, Érica said, stops drinking. Stops smoking. Stops stealing. Stops lying. Stops beating his wife. He finds a job. Puts on weight.

Shit, just look at the down-and-out people who go to Érica's church. I don't see anything but scumbag blacks, I said out loud.

The owner of the hotel looked at me, serious. I turned it off, I didn't want to see Marlênio preach.

Hallelujah, I said before leaving.

It was a nice night, so I went for a walk. Araçariguama's square was empty, there was nothing to do. I sat down on a bench and thought about Marlênio.

Who is Marlênio Silvano? Santana, my partner in the killing business, now dead, had asked.

A preacher, I said.

I know he's a preacher, Santana said, but where'd the guy come from?

That conversation had taken place over ten years ago. And I remembered it all like it was yesterday.

What's his connection to you?

Nothing, I said.

Shit, it can't be nothing, the guy ruined your life, you're messed up, really messed up. The investigator from the sixteenth just called me, Santana said, and told me you're in deep shit. That Marlênio went to the precinct yesterday with a broken arm, just out of the hospital. Marlênio went to the precinct to fuck you over. He said the body they found in Marcão's workshop is your wife. He also lodged a complaint against you. And made another serious accusation: that you've been threatening Érica's life. The whole business stinks, Máiquel.

Thinking about all that got me agitated. I needed to beat up on someone, anyone. Smash some idiot's face. I remembered that now I had the telephone number of Érica's house. I could call her. I had a crazy urge to phone Érica and ask how she could have married that guy. Tell her what was going to happen in the coming days. I'm heading for there. You can expect me. I'm coming for my daughter. I'm going to fuck Marlênio but good.

I returned to the hotel, entering quietly so as not to disturb Eunice, and got the envelope that Jonas had given me. I went back to the square and the pay phone. Hello? Dona Érica, please. A minute later she came to the phone. Shit. I hung up. I wasn't about to make it that easy for her.

I called again. She herself answered. What kind of joke is this? she asked. Who is it? Hello? Hello?

I hung up. I knew Érica. She wouldn't sleep that night.

I woke up early and went to the clinic.

Your dog had a good night, Paula said when I arrived.

He stared at me, his mouth open, his tongue hanging out. He looked like a wreck.

I helped take his temperature, give him serum, bathe him. Paula thought Tiger must be about five years old. And that if he hadn't been run over he'd have soon starved to death. He was lucky he found you, she said. Tiger looked at me, seeming to smile.

I didn't have anything to do except stay there with Tiger. I ended up helping Paula take care of the other animals. I held them for her to examine and bathed a couple of basset hounds.

What is it you do? she asked.

I sell pills, I said.

And your wife?

I'm not married, I replied. She liked hearing that, I noticed. Do you have a boyfriend? I asked.

We had a fight, she answered. He's very jealous.

A good reason to come back to Araçariguama in the future, I thought.

I met Eunice back at the hotel at lunchtime. She was all excited about the outing she'd gone on through the city and had discovered that nearby there was the Bible museum. They even have a Bible from caveman days. Don't you want to go there?

I told her she could go by herself, I'd rather stay with Tiger.

Forgive me, said Eunice. I was nasty to you yesterday.

In the afternoon, she decided to go to the clinic with me. Did you see Dr Clog? she asked on the way.

I didn't know what she was talking about.

You'd think you hadn't even noticed the size of her clogs, said Eunice mockingly. I never saw anybody come to work in clogs, clop, clop. Just to attract attention. And I also never saw white pants as tight as those. You'll excuse me, Máiquel, but a serious doctor doesn't do things like that. Only here. And I'll even bet you think she's pretty. You were drooling over her like an idiot. Men are so stupid.

Eunice was itching for a fight. She was just waiting for an opportunity. Luckily, Paula wasn't at the clinic. Tiger wagged his tail when he saw me. He looked at us in such a way that he didn't even seem like a dog, he seemed like a man who'd been transformed into a dog after dropping acid.

I have the impression, I told Eunice, that one day Tiger will turn back into a man. I mean, if we give him more acid.

Eunice had never done acid and didn't get the joke.

Doesn't it look like he's laughing? I asked. Good dog.

He's so ugly it hurts, said Eunice. I never saw anything like it.

At the end of the afternoon, we returned to the hotel. We had dinner right there.

Before going to sleep, I went to the pay phone and called Érica's house again.

The Bishop is at the church, said the maid.

Tell her that her friend called.

What friend? the woman asked.

Just tell her that, her friend.

The next day, I left Eunice at the hotel having breakfast and went to the clinic to get Tiger.

Paula was waiting for me. Wet hair, wearing sneakers. I'm going to the beach, she said, to get some sun.

I thought about saying something, beach, sun, but didn't have anything to say.

Let's do some shopping, she said. Tiger is going to need things for the trip.

You've been very good to the two of us, I said as we walked to a nearby store.

Take that blanket, vitamins, ah, and this nursing bottle too, he's not managing to eat properly.

Then we went to a pharmacy and bought serum and medicines.

We went back to the clinic. Paula helped me place Tiger in the back seat. I think he's comfortable, she said. Here's my cellphone number, she said, handing me her card. Give me a call now and then and fill me in.

It was already ten when I picked Eunice up at the hotel. It was sunny. Tiger seemed calm. I just hope he doesn't vomit, she said.

If everything went well, in twelve hours I'd be in Campo Grande.

6

The first thing my father taught me was that I was invisible. And the second was that I was worthless. And that nothing mattered. He taught me in his own way, without saying a word, just with his eyes, while everything around us rotted. A can of worms. I learned fast. When I go anywhere, if I see a lot of people it festers in me that I'm the worst. And I leave. Sometimes I don't even go in. Máiquel, come over here, people say. I don't go. I run away. I hide. Funny, what you think about on the highway. The connections. You think about one thing because you've thought about another. I'm invisible. No one sees me. For a long time that was bad. Now it's good.

A long time before I returned to São Paulo, after Érica ran away, right after everything fell part, when my picture was appearing in newspapers, when TV and radio were talking about me, when cops were everywhere, looking for me,

I thought I'd never again be able to know what it was to go out into the street, invisible, anonymous, free, without anyone pursuing me, jerking my chain. I couldn't even go down to the corner. And when everything got even worse, I had to bury myself somewhere in a series of hideouts, locked in for months at a time, looking through a hole in the roof, with my revolver always under the pillow. I thought my life would never go back to normal.

It took a long time for me to be nothing again and to learn that Brazil is an immense hole where no one can find you if you don't want them to. The truth is, nobody sees you. You can come out into the open. All you have to do is wait for them to forget. And it doesn't take long. Because the truth is you aren't worth anything. That was how I felt that day, on the Castelo Branco highway, at sixty miles per hour. A nothing. Wide lane. A long trip. Another four hundred miles to Campo Grande.

You're missing out, Eunice, there's lots of signs to read.

Shh, now she wanted to sleep.

She wasn't worth anything either, Eunice. Neither of us. What did the world want with us? Nothing.

We had lunch at a barbecue place at the entrance to Bauru.

Eunice was happy because she'd called her brother's cellular from a pay phone. I think he's going to meet us in Campo Grande, she said. He's near here, delivering a load of lumber. Odécio was his name. Odécio's really cool, she said.

I heard lots of stories about Odécio. He must be a crook. I had even had a dream about Odécio's Scania 112 HW. The cabin was all in gold. I told Eunice about it over lunch.

She laughed. Know something? she said. The two of you are going to be great friends.

I liked hearing that. Liked it but didn't believe it.

When we left, while Eunice was in the bathroom, I gave Tiger some water. You're gonna be okay, you big mutt. You're gonna go around with me sniffing women's snatches. Tiger was very sharp. He knew what I was saying. That's right, I repeated. Snatch. Arf, arf. You're gonna stick that cracked head of yours into the snatch of chicks and tell me if it's worth the trouble. It even seemed like he wanted to answer, Tiger. I fixed his medicine in the nursing bottle, but the problem was that the poor thing didn't have the strength for anything.

Eunice returned in a hurry, carrying a newspaper. Let's go, now, she said. We got in the car. Máiquel, isn't it you in this photo? she asked, pointing to a story in the *Diário do Estado*. Me, blond, in an article about the death of a cop. A picture of Bruno. Isn't that the guy I saw at your house?

Pictures of other killers wanted by the police. Uh oh. It was all starting again. They told my story one more time. *The vigilante of São Bernardo*. Blah-blah-blah. Divani also appeared in the article, tying together the facts. That irritated me; Divani had no need to shoot off her mouth. *Professional killer. A fugitive for ten years. An assassination business* ... I didn't have the patience to read it all and skipped over entire parts.

I started the motor and got onto the highway.

Máiquel, answer me. Is it true? Eunice asked.

Of course not.

You had a business, she said.

A security business, I replied. An asset.

That Bruno guy was at your house. Did you kill him?

I get upset when I'm bombarded with questions, I can't think straight, lose my bearings. All those guys, I said, were friends of mine. I helped everybody, Eunice. All that bunch.

Eunice went on talking about the paper, about my bleached hair, but I wasn't listening anymore. Everything's okay, I thought. All I have to do is keep on ahead. Campo Grande, three hundred and ninety-four miles, the sign said. Another eight hours of travel, maybe nine, and I'd be there. In any case, this time nothing would stop me. The photo was an old one: would I be recognized? In the rearview mirror I looked like someone else. Dark, with longer hair. Older. Thinner. And, after all, it wasn't the first time I'd been in a story like that in the newspapers. Every time there was some massacre, I'd noticed, with a lot of people killed, they'd right away bring up my name. But later they'd forget again. They'd forgotten before, they'd forget again. That story, that newspaper, none of it mattered. And anyway, nobody read newspapers, that's for sure.

When I turned my attention back to Eunice she was still babbling on. Isn't Divani, that black woman, your neighbor? You see what you get for getting mixed up with tramps? Eunice lost it when she was jealous. Tiger started barking.

Take it easy, Eunice.

Did you screw that black woman? What else don't I know? That black bitch, she said. That dirty black bitch.

Why don't you get your backpack and go home to Nova Iguaçu? I said.

And you, why don't you stop screwing up? she replied. Ever since I met you, no sign of looking for a job. Killing a cop. Even a retard knows that's pure shit.

At that moment, Tiger vomited.

Damn it, Eunice said, not even the dog is any good. That cripple is going to mean work for me.

Leave it, I'll clean it up, I said.

I pulled over to the side of the road. Eunice violently grabbed Tiger, who yelped in pain.

Let go of him, I shouted, put my dog down, don't do that

You ought to feel sorry for Bruno, she answered, not for some flea-bitten dog.

You don't know what you're talking about, I said.

I can read, she replied. I read the newspaper. I know very well what I'm talking about.

I'm going to leave you at the bus station, I said.

Sure, she said, now that I know who you are. You and that black woman. And me and Bruno. Was that why you killed him?

I was angry at Eunice, felt like slapping her pallid cheek.

I got the blanket and cleaned up the vomit, which stank like hell, and threw everything away. I opened the trunk, took a wool shirt from the backpack, and set Tiger on top of it.

Disgusting, said Eunice, a dog's a dog, and people are people. You ought to learn to separate the two.

I don't separate them, I said. To me a dog is people and people are dogs.

She went to the trunk and took out her things. You can go

on, she said, I'm going to hitchhike. I don't feel like traveling with a killer.

I got out of the car. Eunice, it's dangerous on the highway. Get in, I'll take you to the bus station.

What's dangerous is traveling with you. Why didn't you tell me before just what you were? What else don't I know, Máiquel? That you rape women? Kill children?

Get in, I ordered. I was pushing her inside the car, forcibly.

No doubt you rob banks too. You think you can order me around? Think I'm afraid of you?

I pushed her into the car. Whap, I got slapped in the face.

Jesus, what an irritating woman.

Get out, I ordered. I had wasted a lot of time driving into Bauru and looking for the bus station, and now Eunice didn't want to go back to Nova Iguaçu.

I'm not going to leave Tiger in this condition, she said. He's sick.

The dog is mine, I answered. Get out.

Eunice wouldn't move. She was looking at her fingernails. I parked, opened the car door, got her things and put everything on the sidewalk.

Get out. I took money from my wallet and stuck it in one of the pockets in Eunice's backpack. This ought to be enough to get you back home. Leave, go away.

You're mean, she said. I'm not the kind of person who abandons a sick animal. She closed the door.

All right, I said. I put her bags back in the trunk. But listen up, I said when I got back in the car, I'm the one who decides things around here. If you want to leave, you'll have to wait till the next stop, and I decide where that's going to be. Understood?

That black woman, grumbled Eunice, I'm sure you screwed that woman. Absolutely sure. You just can't keep it in your pants, can you?

The dog can't come in, said the young man at the reception desk at the Alvorada Inn Hotel in Birigüi.

I was exhausted and didn't want to go out looking for some other place to sleep. My eyes burned. I slid a ten across the counter. Our dog is very sick, I explained.

Two minutes later, we were carrying Tiger upstairs.

We want separate beds, Eunice said. We're not married. And then, trying to charm the man, she asked if Birigüi wasn't the name of an endangered species of monkey.

He didn't know anything, the hotel employee. I'm new here, he said.

I made Tiger comfortable in the bathroom, gave him his fluid, his tonic, mashed up some dog biscuits with water. He ate a little, vomited, and went to sleep.

I took a shower, and as I was getting ready to leave, Eunice asked me if I wouldn't like to have a pizza.

You eat it, I said. I didn't want to talk to Eunice. I knew how she worked. Eunice loved to start an argument.

Have you ever noticed, she'd said in bed the other day, how I like to fight? I've been like that since I was little. Something gets lit up inside me, a fire, a light, I don't know what it is, all I know is that it's a bad sign, and right away I go from positive to negative. After it erupts, there's no way around it, better get out of the line of fire or you'll catch some of it. The other day, I slapped a woman who was going out with Odécio. She said something stupid like 'our Scania,' and I slapped her in the face twice, and my brother took one too, for trying to stop me. The woman left there whimpering. That's just who I am, she said. I'm dying to get my hands on that Érica woman, that child-kidnapper is going to get a piece of my mind.

In São Paulo, Eunice had fought with clerks in stores, with street vendors, with waitresses, it was hell. Afterwards she would regret it and go all soft. Now she wanted to have pizza with me, after calling me a murderer for almost a hundred and fifty miles.

I left some money on top of the TV and went out. She could have dinner by herself.

I went to a pay phone and called Érica's house. An answering machine with a young girl's voice picked up. My mother, my father, and I are out. Leave a message after the tone, and may God be with you. It was her, Samantha. I hung up. I called again. And then once more. My father. The 'my father' was Marlênio. That enraged me.

Érica and Samantha were covering me with sand, at the beach. It was sunny.

What are you doing? asked the ice-cream vendor.

We're burying my father.

We laughed.

Wake up, Máiquel. I was suspicious that the ice-cream vendor was a cop in disguise. I had my revolver. I tried to move, but there was too much sand, they'd overdone it. That's what comes, I thought, from allowing everything. There have to be limits. I felt confused with all that sand on top of me. I think they're really trying to bury me, I thought. Wake up, Máiquel.

I jumped out of bed, my heart racing. I was covered with sweat, an awful sensation, I didn't know where I was. Birigüi. Hotel. Eunice. It took me a few seconds to orientate myself.

Shit, said Eunice, give me a hand here, I think Tiger is dying.

The rest of the night was agony. We took the dog to a veterinarian emergency room. You never should have removed him from the clinic, the doctor said, after we told him Tiger's complete history. He's very weak.

The prediction was that he would have to stay there for two days, on intravenous. Hearing that made me sad, 'cause it seemed like Tiger understood everything.

Why don't we leave him here, suggested Eunice, go to Campo Grande, settle accounts with that child-robber, and then come back for him?

Like I was going to come back to Birigüi. Or leave Tiger by himself.

At 4 a.m., before going to the hotel, I called Érica again. The recording with Samantha's voice came on. They must be traveling, Eunice said. Didn't Jonas say they have a country place near Campo Grande?

The next two days, while waiting for Tiger to get better, I called Érica several times, but there was never anyone at home. The recording with Samantha's voice also didn't come on anymore.

I called Jonas. Can you find out the phone number of Érica's house in the country?

He said he could. Call back tomorrow, he said.

On Monday, Tiger looked much better. Now he can travel, the vet said.

I called Jonas before hitting the highway and he told me he hadn't been able to find the phone number of Marlênio's place. Son of a bitch. At Érica's home no one answered. Shit. Fuck. Goddamn. Nothing I could do but cuss.

It was seven in the morning, and I wanted to make it to Campo Grande before two in the afternoon.

7

Blazing sun. A truck selling bananas on the highway.

What day was your daughter born? Eunice asked when she got tired of remaining silent.

I didn't remember the date anymore. It was at the beginning of the year, I said, but I don't know the date. I don't pay attention to those things, I said. Christmas, New Year's.

And what do you plan to say to her when you meet?

I preferred not to think about those details. It made me nervous. My plan was just to go to Campo Grande, and after that everything was a blur, things would happen, I knew that, but all I was certain of was what I'd do to Marlênio's mug. What to say to Samantha?

The problem, Eunice said, isn't you going after your daughter now, the problem is you didn't do it earlier. When Érica ran away and took Samantha with her, you should have taken a stance.

Actually, the problem was my picture in the newspaper. Me and the other killers. Bruno the cop. Yeah, that's what my problem was. Whether they dragged out the subject, whether they took a long time to forget. Killers wanted by the police. I didn't want to prolong the matter with Eunice and talk a lot of nonsense. I tried to explain to her that tiny details, dotting every *i*, crossing every *t*, just mess up your thoughts, whether it's going to be this way or that way, whether I'm going to say this or that to my daughter is stupid, I said, what matters is that –

That's idiotic, Eunice interrupted. You have to think about everything. You're her father. A twelve-year-old can reason. A father who disappears for ten years is a father who doesn't give a damn. You have to say something, Eunice insisted. You have to explain. And besides, that kidnapper, if she told Samantha that you're her father, she told her in the worst possible way. She must not have told her; Jonas said the girl was registered with Marlênio's name, didn't he? Why, Máiquel, why did you wait so long to look for your daughter?

I'm a fugitive, I felt like saying, but I didn't say anything. I saw that Eunice was getting nervous again. To tell the truth, I said something worse. Érica, I said, is a good mother.

Érica, Eunice replied, irritated, is a kidnapper. You don't steal a father's child. She's an idiot, that Érica. Immoral. Máiquel, what are we going to do in Campo Grande? I hope you get your daughter and we can go back to Nova Iguaçu. My brother's said he can help you. It's a start. Now there's that newspaper saying things about you. You say it's all lies.

And I believe you. Tell me if I'm wrong. What I hate in life is wasting time. Being played for a fool. Look at that sign: *Careful, you may be stepping on the cure for cancer.* What do you suppose they have here that cures cancer, huh, Máiquel? Like that, on the highway?

It was good when Eunice went back to reading road signs. At least she had that going for her. It wouldn't take long for her to recover her good mood.

In Castilho, near Jupiá, there was a crowd of people along the riverbank. Traffic was slow, I thought there'd been an accident, but then I saw that everybody was carrying bags.

Must be the cure for cancer, Eunice said.

They're catching fish, a woman in the car beside us said, there's catfish everywhere.

A man in water up to his shins was clubbing an enormous fish that was there only because the level of the dam was so low.

Wanna buy some? asked a boy, coming up to us. It's *piapara.* There's *curimbatá* too.

A pile of fish was tossed into the woods. Nobody buys that, the boy told Eunice, when she asked if it was also for sale.

I became uneasy; it wouldn't be long before the police showed up. It's shit like this that nails you, I thought. I maneuvered away from the jam and went along the apron till I made it to the clear lane ahead.

Três Lagoas, Arapuá, we moved on. Eunice asked if I wanted her to drive. I didn't know she drove. One more reason for you to marry me, she said. Eunice never gave up.

I jumped into the backseat, put Tiger's head in my lap, and slept the rest of the way.

This is the watchman, there's nobody home, said the voice at the other end of the line. Eunice was taking a shower, and I had just fed Tiger.

From the bed I could see the hotel's water tanks. From that position, in fact, I could see a lot of them, scattered around the neighborhood. There was no lack of water tanks in Campo Grande.

The room was stuffy. I took off my shirt and turned on the fan.

Jonas hadn't said anything about watchmen at Érica's house. Could the guy be from some firm? An armed watchman? Or was he just some poor devil hired off the streets? As a rule, a watchman is just that, a nobody who doesn't know anything and who stays at somebody else's house not doing shit. In the days when I had the security firm, we used to hire a bunch of small-time criminals to handle that service. Lots of times they would hold up our future clients, who would later pay us to rid them of the robbers.

In any case, a watchman could make things hard for me. Some of those guys carry weapons and shoot to kill. Sometimes they hit their target. The chances of that happening aren't all that great. A dog works better if you want to do injury to a criminal, but a security guy can still do a lot of damage.

I decided I wouldn't go there till the next day. There wasn't any hurry. At least Érica was still in town. That was a relief. I started thinking, over the weekend, when they didn't answer the phone, that she'd run away. No, she was still there, and I was going to see my daughter, it was just a matter of time. I would catch Érica when she was coming out of the house. I was going to get Marlênio too, he'd be first. Calmly. I was going to look everything over, beforehand. Nothing hasty, I decided.

Eunice came out of the shower, wrapped in a towel. I'm going to call Odécio, she said happily.

After she spoke to her brother, who was already in Campo Grande and would meet us the next day, I told her about the watchman.

Of course, she said, a child-snatcher, owner of a church, has to have a gunman. Those people are bad news. Eunice was fragrant. She kissed me. We haven't fucked for two days, she said. That's a record, you know?

I pushed Eunice toward the bed. Shit, that mixture of the smell of pussy and soap was driving me crazy.

Do you love me? she asked while we were fucking.

I don't remember saying anything.

You did, she said, yes you did, Eunice said, yessir, you said you loved me. It was the first time you admitted it, she said as she was getting dressed.

We went out for something to eat. It was a hot night and Odécio, who knew Campo Grande well, had told us to go to Feirona, an enormous field full of stalls where you can get anything. There Eunice bought some handicraft things. It's to decorate our house, she said. Isn't that cool?

We chose a table, she ordered alligator meat. She wanted to try everything the waiter recommended. Your problem, Máiquel, is you're very stubborn. Didn't you hear what the man said? Only here in Campo Grande can you get *chipa*. Eat it, it's cheese bread. Order Paraguayan soup. It's pudding, don't you like pudding? You don't like anything. You're a real drag. All you do is drink Coca-Cola all day long. That stuff burns a hole in your stomach, did you know that? You know the difference between us?

Yeah, I do, I answered. The difference is that I've killed a lot of people. I'm a fugitive, I said.

Silence.

Everything you read in the paper was true, I said. I mean, not everything. A large part. There's a lot of lies too. But I was a vigilante. A killer. Whatever name they call that shit. It was a long time ago. Today I'm a fugitive.

What about that cop? Eunice asked.

It's true, I said. I killed the cop. He was trying to arrest me.

Eunice stared at me, not having the heart to ask more questions. We walked back to the hotel in silence.

Are you going to change your way of life? she asked when we got to the room.

I'm not going to join a church, I said. And I'm not going to prison.

Eunice smiled, an empty, awkward smile. Then she sat on the bed and took off her shoes. We stretched out.

I want you to tell me everything, she said, everything. I really love you, Máiquel.

Forgive me, I said, but I'm not going to tell anything. I couldn't take any more of that story.

I turned my back and went to sleep.

*   *   *

My car was parked at the corner. I spent a good part of the morning waiting, watching the movement. No one entered, no one left, everything was very quiet.

It was almost noon before I noticed. Practically all the houses had put out their garbage, except Érica's. When we lived in São Bernardo, Érica was so worried about garbage that she would sometimes phone downstairs to the doorman and ask, How many bags today, Rosalino?

A hundred and two, he'd say. A hundred and seven. A hundred and nine. That was the average.

Érica had nothing to do with the garbage, but she couldn't help but be interested. At first she only asked about our building. Then, when she would go for a stroll with Samantha, she started talking to the neighboring doormen. What's the average number of bags of garbage you produce?

I thought that business of 'produce' was funny.

But that's just what it is, she said. Garbage isn't like bananas, growing out of the ground. At Christmas, the number doubles, Máiquel. There's a lot of trash in the world. We're going to drown in garbage.

Érica was one of the ones who produced the most garbage.

That day, though, there was no bag at the door of her house. That was what woke me up. I went nearer. Through the front window I could see the living room was empty. There was no one living in the house. I rang the bell, to check if the watchman was inside. Nothing.

I pushed against the door. Getting in that way wouldn't be

easy. I went around to the back and managed to squeeze through the kitchen window after breaking the glass with a rock.

The house was vacated and cleaned. Nothing but empty boxes. It hadn't been long since they abandoned the place. YOU'RE VERY SPECIAL was written on a poster of a little girl hugging a kitten. In the closet I found a doll with only one leg and a calendar taped beside the mirror. I went to the kitchen, got a box and put everything in it.

Then I went to the bedroom. The lace curtains were still there. The closet, empty. In a drawer, a few church pamphlets. *How much to offer to the Lord? The example, worker, is the widow's mite. It was she who pleased the Lord. For she gave all she had.* Another pamphlet. Iara, the Indian from the rainforest who found her true love. Summarizing, Iara lived in the depths of the rainforest until Pedro arrived in an airplane to speak of Christ's love for everyone who lived there. A drawing. *Help bring the Bible to Iara.* Words in the form of a cross. Four letters each, GIVE, LOVE.

I gathered up the pamphlets, stuck them in the box, and left.

The doll with one leg was on Eunice's stomach. The two of us, holding hands, in bed, silent. I asked if she was hungry.

I'm going to take a shower, she said, then we'll see.

While Eunice was in the shower, I stretched out on the floor beside Tiger and looked at the pamphlets from Érica's church. One of them was about forgiveness. *Get your Bible and ask for forgiveness*, was written. *It doesn't matter what you've done. Seek out your mother. Your brother. Whomever you have offended. Go to them and say, In the name of the Lord, I come to ask forgiveness.* That way, I thought, it's real easy to be good. You go around screwing up and then you get the Bible and clean up the blood and ask for forgiveness. Sin by day and beg forgiveness by night. Sin and ask for forgiveness, endlessly. The circle of evil. Screw up and apologize. Get fat and then lose weight. The really hard thing was to be good without God. To stay thin without dieting. Good without the Bible. Without being able to go back and ask for forgiveness. Without pills. Because there's no such thing as forgiveness. Because there's no one up there to grant forgiveness, and that's the truth. Only the sky. Totally empty. Filled with stars. That's what the scientists say. So who can you ask for forgiveness?

Eunice came out of the bathroom saying she'd rather get something to eat at the bakery next to the hotel. We had a sandwich and a Coke.

Eunice looked pretty, in a light-blue skirt and white blouse.

You look nice, I said. I felt like she wanted me to say something.

I'm leaving with Odécio, she said. I'm going back to Nova Iguaçu. I think it's better, she said. You know, Máiquel, if you promise me –

But I thought it best to stop her right there. That promise business isn't my thing. I don't make promises. I knew where that line was heading. Fine, I said. Eunice went on talking, which kind of irritated me. She thought I was sad, but I was just irritated.

The sadness came later, much later, when I was already far away.

I liked Eunice. I didn't want her to leave. I could've asked her to stay. But I am the way I am. I don't like asking anyone for anything.

8

Five after seven in the morning. Car horns and confusion. Mothers screwing up traffic, double-parking to dump their kids at school. Me there, at the corner of Samantha's school, watching everything, with Tiger sleeping on the bench beside me. Until a week earlier, Tiger looked like a skinhead. Now that the hair was growing back, the animal was even uglier. I'm going to shave you again, you mutt. Wake up, Tiger. He sleeps all day. Impressive. Eats and sleeps. And farts. And snores. What good is it to go around with a fart-bucket like you, always conked out?

Samantha in a ballet outfit. Samantha holding hands with Érica, entering the church. Samantha and Érica, walking a poodle. Érica had really transformed herself; the Érica that I knew would never have a poodle, that disgusting breed with pompoms and all.

I had been parked at the corner of the Evangelical Education Institute, on rua das Américas, for almost forty

73

minutes, looking at the paper that Jonas had given me. And waiting.

Suddenly, Samantha got out of a car, carrying a backpack.

I quickly jumped out of the car, my legs shaky. I ran toward the entrance gate to get a closer look. The security guard didn't like it and stepped into my path. Only then did I see. It wasn't Samantha. Very different from the girl in the photo. Taller. Heavier. And uglier. No, it's nothing, I told the guard.

I'd been like that since arriving in Campo Grande. I thought every twelve-year-old girl was Samantha.

I stayed there until they closed the gates. I wasn't going to give up.

I decided to look around. I wandered about the city. I already knew the layout of Campo Grande. Beach, mountains, river, there's nothing there; it's just what the name says, one big endless meadow. And there are lots of pharmacies too. Which isn't unusual in this country. Any city you go to has a bunch of pharmacies. And warehouses, vacant lots, slums, people piled on top of one another, traffic jams, dirt, concrete and ugliness. A crazy quilt. The same materials. Concrete blocks, railings, everything unfinished. There's always a sack of cement in the garage, in the living room, in the bedroom of the ones who aren't so badly off, the poor, the wage earners, a bit of sand too. To expand a little more. Upward, sideways, on the lamp posts, on the walls, a pile of wires, stuff written, hanging, ads, plaques, a war zone. They're always adding on, stealing electricity, increasing like worms, procreating, the city is a sickness.

Growing. One more floor, one more room, one more fence, one more garage, and when you look, they've taken over the entire hillside, the field, the beach, covered everything with their ugliness, and it's not only Brazil, no, elsewhere too the rotten part is all alike. On television you can't tell one from the next. When they blow up. In war. They're all the same. Cement and blood. On the pavement. All just the same.

What does this place remind you of? Eunice would ask when we drove into a new city. The truth is that if you're dropped in some city without knowing which it is, you'll never find out where you are. It could be anywhere. Baghdad. Botucatu. Belford Roxo. The same ugliness. The same poverty. It doesn't remind you of anywhere, she herself would answer.

At first Campo Grande impressed me. It looked magnificent, but later I saw that really it was dull. I prefer Nova Iguaçu with Eunice to Campo Grande without Eunice. Birigüi with Eunice to Campo Grande without Eunice. Eunice made cities better. Birigüi, São Bernardo, everything was better when Eunice was at my side. The truth is that I needed Eunice. The truth is that Campo Grande didn't have anything beyond those big avenues; you arrived there and became impressed with those wide streets, but once you passed the first traffic lights, you saw very quick that it ended right there, it was nothing. Campo Grande was one big let-down. At least if Eunice was with me, I thought, I'd go to the Golden Bull, eat meat with manioc flour and drink beer, but by myself what fun was it? Without Eunice, I didn't have any appetite; for two days now I'd eaten nothing but bananas and chocolate.

Buy your sweetheart a cellphone. I went to a shopping mall in Campo Grande just to take a look and have something to talk about with Eunice. You'd love the stores here, I planned to say later when I called her. *Ten installments of thirty-two.* They wanted real bad for me to buy you a cellphone, I would say. They practically twisted my arm. Actually, I only went there because I wanted to call Eunice. I was dying of loneliness.

Hi, she said when she answered, but it was a different hi, cold. Eunice seemed like a stone.

I asked if she'd had a good trip.

Great, she said. What do you want? she asked.

I felt awkward, talked about the stores, but she didn't give a damn.

There's stores everywhere, she said. There's no shortage of stores.

I ate alligator meat, I said. That was a lie. It's horrible, I said. I don't know why you like it.

Listen here, Máiquel, if you have something important to say to me, fine, I'll be very happy. I really want you to call and say something, something real, if you understand me. But don't call me to talk about alligators. And she hung up in my face.

It made me enormously sad to talk with Eunice. I almost called her back to say I was sorry.

I wandered around a while before deciding to go to the Park of the Nations. Tiger was better, I saw that morning. We stretched out in the sun, the two of us, and stayed there, killing time.

At noon, I was in front of the school again. I parked and this time got out of the car immediately, to see everything from up close. I recognized one of Samantha's friends coming out of the building with her mother. It was one of the girls from the photo Jonas had given me.

Is Samantha inside? I asked.

She looked at me, startled. Not the girl, her mother. Her daughter smiled at me, without denying or affirming. The mother hurriedly positioned herself at the steering wheel.

The problem, I thought, is my clothes. Fathers dress a certain way. Just by looking at me she knew I was something else, a spy, an intruder, a fugitive. My pants, my shirt were nothing like the pants and shirts of the people there; theirs were the way they should be, with creases, made of linen, ties, father clothes, the clothes of a lawyer, dentist, businessman, a belt that went with the shoes, dress shirt, blue, pink, beige, there was even one clown in a blazer despite the heat. I remembered my own time as a clown, two-tone shoes, checkered shirt; I looked like a fag in my business clothes. They were dirty now, my pants, from rolling on the grass with Tiger. At least the rest was clean, I thought. My hands.

I almost asked the doorman for information, but I thought that might raise suspicions. No rush, I thought. That was my motto.

I returned to the car. I looked at the paper Jonas had given me. Four o'clock, guitar lesson, at the church. I still had time to spare.

Before going back to the hotel, I stopped at a supermarket and bought bananas, chocolate, and Coca-Cola.

I can't leave here, Jonas said when I phoned to tell him what had happened. Do this, write down Anderson's number, he's a detective. Anderson is a friend of mine, he lives in Campo Grande and will do whatever it takes to help you.

Anderson wasn't in his office, so I left a message on his answering machine. It's urgent, I said.

I watched TV until three o'clock, with Tiger sleeping and farting beside me. Prrrrrrrrrrr. He didn't seem at all bothered by his farts, prrrrrrrrrrr, he even liked them, 'cause he would stick his nose in his butt. The truth is that I couldn't give the dog any more chocolate. Or Coca-Cola.

At three-thirty I was parked on Visconde de Albuquerque, across from a large building covered with asbestos shingles. That's how Protestant churches are, they look like building-supply stores, supermarkets, shopping centers, movie theaters. It's all about serious money. On the façade, a drawing of a heart surrounded by thorns. Church of the Powerful Heart of Jesus was written in neon. Of course by then Érica knew about me. Knew I was there after her and my daughter. She hadn't changed homes by accident. But letting go of everything, of that gold mine, was a different story. She was no fool, neither was Marlênio.

This is exactly what I was thinking when a large jerk in a suit came up to the car. Tiger started barking.

Is there something you want? he asked.

I came to speak to the pastor, I said.

What pastor?

Pastor Marlênio.

There's nobody here today, he said.

Not Miss Érica either?

Nobody. They're traveling.

I'm a music teacher. Miss Érica told me to look for the guitar teacher at four o'clock today.

The man was undecided. I told him a pack of lies.

By then I had read almost all the pamphlets about missions, which is what they called starting up new churches throughout Brazil. I said that Pastor Marlênio was thinking of me for a mission.

Naturally he'd been warned not to give information to strangers. But as soon as I came up with that talk about missions the guy forgot everything. He liked me.

You're going, huh? Where to?

Awful breath, worse than Tiger's. The man asked a lot of questions. He told me about his stupid little life there. Opening and closing doors. He'd just brought his family down from the north.

Wherever they send me. I'm going to preach the word of the Lord. So? Can I go inside?

Not with the dog, he said finally.

He can stay in the car, I said.

That was when I screwed up. I asked if Samantha had come to class that afternoon. It did no good for me to explain that I'd given the girl private lessons, that I visited the family often.

You better leave, he said, and the situation deteriorated.

It always causes problems when you rush things. I was mad as hell at myself.

I went back to the car and, later, watched the students as they came out. Samantha wasn't among them.

On the way back to the hotel, I drove by a park where they were preparing for the June festivities. I got out to watch. An enormous bonfire was going to be lit, forty feet high.

I bought sausages from a cart and gave them to Tiger. We sat down and watched the activities. I like bonfires.

After a time, a girl came and sat down beside me. Short skirt, nice legs. She was pretty all over. Real pretty.

What's your name?

Máiquel, I replied.

Like the singer, she said, the one in the couple that's going to sing this weekend. Maicon and Marlon.

Mine is Máiquel, I said, like Máiquel Jackson.

Ah, she said. There's also going to be a Laura and Aurélio show, you like them?

I didn't know who they were but I said I liked them.

What a coincidence, she said. I love them. Airo and Rhuan, Tostão and Guarani, it's going to be a good evening. Campo Grande is like that, she said, very lively.

Her name was Sílvia and she had green eyes. I'm always suspicious of very pretty women. Actually, I'm afraid. There are men who love going around with a knockout babe on their arm. I hate it. A woman that everyone wants to screw. What's the advantage? Everybody looks, covets, comments, wants to grab her. Just thinking about it gives me a headache. That type of woman doesn't even turn me on.

I'm not from Campo Grande, she said. I'm a receptionist. But I want to be a model, she said. Aren't you going to buy me a drink?

We headed for a bar, but I wasn't into it. I'm immune to gorgeous women. They won't nail me.

The bar was pretty shabby. For her to see I wasn't impressed by those killer green eyes.

Sílvia wanted beer. I thought she was going to leave right away, but I was wrong.

Your dog is really ugly, she said.

We ended up in bed.

Sílvia told me her story, a very sad one. After her mother died, when she was fourteen, her father traded her to a neighbor for a cow. Besides everything else, the cow was sick, she said. It died right after the swap. And my father was weak, he didn't even have the courage to complain. He was afraid of getting shot. Her 'new owner' was a farmer, a bad man, who abused her every day until she managed to run away, three years ago. He didn't just abuse her. She was forced to wash, iron, scrub, till the soil, cook, plant, weed, and most of all fuck. Ever since then she's hated men. She dreams about taking a knife and cutting off the farmer's dick. Someday I'm going back there, she said. To kill that son of a bitch. I'd like to kill my father too. Everybody has something in life they dream about. That's mine, to kill those two, she said.

I felt sorry for Sílvia. Where does that farmer live? I asked.

I don't want any help, she said. I want to kill him myself.

That was the last thing I heard. Then I drifted off to sleep.

I woke up the next day to the ringing of the phone. It was Anderson, Jonas's detective friend. We agreed to meet at ten o'clock at his office.

Sílvia had disappeared. She took all the money in my wallet, the whore.

Jonas gave me all the information, Anderson said when I arrived. Everything in his office matched, the desk with the carpet, the chair with the curtains, the ashtray with his tie, the vase with his belt, black, beige, and brown, totally faggoty. If Anderson charges me for the decoration, I thought as he offered me a drink, I'm fucked.

Did you speak to Érica on the phone? he asked, loosening his tie.

I called a few times, I explained, but we didn't talk. Are you a lawyer? I asked.

He laughed. Why? Do I look like a lawyer?

Yeah, I answered. He's vain, I noted. If I told him how I felt about lawyers he wouldn't puff up like that.

My partner wants me to study law, he says I've got a talent for it, he said. Everybody thinks I'm a lawyer. Maybe someday in the future.

Well, he said finally, getting down to cases, it looks like Érica knew you were coming. In his way of dressing, Anderson also wasn't anything like Jonas. All starched. He smoothed his polka-dot tie; it must be hell to wear a suit in Campo Grande.

I just need two things, I said. To find out where my daughter is. And fast.

Anderson agreed to get me some information as soon as possible and asked me to 'vanish.' You could get in the way of my work, he said. Leave it to me, let me do everything.

I left and went directly to Érica's house.

At the door there was a sign: *For Rent*. I went around and entered through the broken glass. Not even the empty boxes were in the kitchen anymore. And the house was cleaner still. Someone had been there.

I went through all the closets and drawers in search of some clue. The only thing of use that I found was the name of the real-estate firm and the agent. *Sol Azul Real Estate, Abílio Paiva.*

I went next door and rang the doorbell. A fat woman answered.

Hi, I said, sorry to bother you. I had an appointment with Abílio, the agent from Sol Azul Real Estate, but he's running late. I need to leave a note for him. Can I leave it with you?

Are you going to rent the house? she asked.

Yes. We're going to be neighbors.

I wrote a note: *The documents are with Marcelo. I'll come by at two tomorrow. Thanks, Leandro.*

What's your name? I asked.

Teresa.

What a nice name. Mine is Leandro. Would you give this to Abílio, Teresa? He'll stop by here, all you have to do is give him this note.

Teresa was very helpful. Her cheeks were glowing.

I thanked her and, as I was leaving, asked if she minded giving me her phone number.

I work here, she said, after handing me the number. It's better to call at night, it's easier. Because of the woman I work for.

Better yet, I said, if you have a free weekend, you can do some work at my place, I'm going to need somebody to help out. Can I call you?

At noon, I was back at the school gate. This time, I had no sooner parked than the security guard came to talk to me. You can't stop here, he said.

There's no sign, I answered.

We save this space for the students' parents.

This is a public area, I said.

I know, but could you please go and sleep somewhere else?

I just want some information.

The man looked at me. I wrote down your license number, he said. Get out of here before I call the police.

It was a lousy day. At the church it was even worse. I waited until the time for the service and went in with the people. But those evangelicals are tough.

Immediately two women came up to me. We're helpers, they said, The pastor would like a word with you.

The security guard from the day before wasn't there.

We went into a room.

Hi, brother, said a guy in a suit. How can we help you?

I'm looking for Marlênio, I explained.

There's no one here by that name, he said.

I laughed.

You were here in our church yesterday, we were told. Unfortunately, the person you're looking for has no connection to our church. Your name's Máiquel, isn't it?

Tell Érica that I want my daughter, I said.

Brother, I don't understand your words.

I was itching to punch out the pastor's lights. The bastard.

When I got back to the hotel, the phone was ringing. It was Anderson. I've got news for you, he said. See how fast I am?

9

I've been thinking about becoming a preacher too, said Anderson. That's where the money is in Brazil. Besides which, you don't need college, it's just blah-blah-blah. If you know how to read and write, the Holy Spirit takes care of the rest.

We were in Anderson's office, him smoking, me listening. I pay a fortune in taxes, he said, while those bastards, those auditorium emcee monkeys, because that's what they are, start out without cameras, without studios, and later they get everything, concessions from the government, they own television. Have you seen the number of religious programs on TV?

I hardly ever turned on the television since Eunice left. Just to watch football. Whiskey, cigarettes, credit card, I used to love seeing those commercials, happy beautiful women wearing jewels, men with a drink in their hand, laughing, full of teeth, smoking, driving huge cars, walking on the beach in white pants, in slow motion, now none of that barely existed anymore. You didn't even see gorgeous women on TV these days. Just executives, housewives worried about economizing. The Ministry of Health warns, they say, that cigarettes cause cancer. That's how it is nowadays. And they offer chicken parts, sirloin steak, butterfly-hunting Barbie dolls, payable in three installments, a sixteen-piece set of glass dinnerware, four plates, three easy installments, and a curtain in raw cotton, pressure cooker, all inexpensive, on time, in twenty or more installments, Casas Bahia never leaves you alone, ugly commercials, ugly people, everything for you and your home, they say. Anybody who doesn't have a home, like me, isn't interested.

To start a sect, Anderson went on, all you need is gall. You go to a notary public and bang, you're a minister. And you don't pay a thing. That's why nowadays you've got a church for every kind of follower, queers, businessmen, surfers, even for those who want to speak to God only in English. You kill two birds with one stone, you talk to God and learn English.

But what about Érica? I asked. Impressive the way Anderson beat around the bush.

Érica's left, and you're wasting your time here in Campo Grande, he said. You can pack your bags and hit the road. She left town four days ago. That bastard of a husband of hers went with her. They sold the country house, which incidentally was the only thing in their own name. Everything else was rented. They disappeared. You were asleep at the switch. You kept phoning, broadcasting that you were on

87

the way. Know something? he said. When we want revenge, our greatest weapon is surprise. It took me a long time to learn the wisdom of the saying that revenge is a dish best eaten cold. When we hold the trumps, the temptation is to right away alert the enemy, I'm gonna fuck you, I hold all the cards. But that's for amateurs. A pro keeps his mouth shut. Silent as the grave. He first lets the grub cool down. He prepares his pounce. And then, when the chow is nice and chilled, that's when he goes to town, because revenge has to be eaten cold. If someone wants to eat it hot, like you, what happens? Nothing. Érica grabs your daughter and takes off. I checked at the school. I checked at the real-estate agency. I saw the telephone bill for the house. Their phone had caller ID. The preacher saw that things were going to get ugly.

Where'd they go? I asked.

We're going to find out soon. I've located the firm that handled the moving.

The conversation ended, and Anderson continued drawing out the matter, talking about the difference between living in Campo Grande and in São Paulo, dumb talk. I just love Jonas, he said. He's like a brother to me. Are you two good friends?

Yes, we are, I lied.

I spent all the next day with Tiger, in the hotel, waiting for news from Anderson. It's true, that story of dogs ending up resembling their masters. Tiger moved around looking down at the ground, just like me. At his paws. Suspicious. And he didn't like noise. You're just like Máiquel, aren't you, you big mutt? Crazy about chocolate. He had another bout of the

88

shits that afternoon, but he didn't seem to give a damn, he'd do anything for a Black Diamond bar.

That night, after cleaning up a lot of Tiger's shit, I decided to call Teresa. It's Leandro, I've rented the house next to yours. Remember me?

She remembered, of course. I asked if the agent had come by.

No, he hadn't.

Would you like to go out for some barbecue? I ventured.

Only if it's after work, she answered.

At nine o'clock she was waiting for me in front of her employer's house.

Teresa's hands were cold, her face oily, and she smiled every time I looked at her. She wore little black boots, jeans below the knee, and a tight red T-shirt that showed her prominent rolls of fat.

She was ill at ease in the restaurant, afraid of the waiters, the silverware, the dishes, the glasses. I was familiar with that feeling, I've often been afraid in my life. After I adopted my motto, 'Fuck you,' everything got easier. I showed her my tattoo, but Teresa didn't understand. Red cheeks. I tried to explain in a different way. The secret, I said, is to hold on tight. Grab onto everything, I said. Life.

She still didn't understand anything.

I told her that was how I got by. Strength. Grab the glasses, the plates. You've got to know how to latch on, I said. It makes all the difference. We can't be soft. People notice it. The waiters. The rich. One secret, I said, is to look hard, inside them. Inside the fuckers. Try it, I said.

But she sat there with her idiotic expression, not asking anything; I think she was used to not understanding dick.

I used to be that way too. In the past. Before they fucked me over. But if you pretend, things change, I said. Because, deep down, they're afraid. The sons of bitches. I thought I could go further with Teresa. Pick up the silverware, I said. I must have shouted, she was startled. I told her, in a lower tone, that it worked for me. Strength.

I remembered Érica asking what I felt the first time I held a gun. I didn't feel anything, I replied. That was a lie, I had felt distress, a shiver, I didn't like guns.

Holding a gun is like putting on boots, she said. Or a crown on your head. It changes everything.

And it had changed everything. Weapons had taught me that. To grab, forcefully. The grip. The crown. In restaurants, I said, I grab the knife, the fork, and stick it into the meat.

My coaching didn't do any good. I gave up. Teresa sat there the entire evening, afraid of the silverware.

But Teresa had one thing going for her, she would answer all the questions I asked her. Yes, she had known the former neighbors well, they were preachers. Dona Érica was a fine person. A bishop, she said. Married to Mr Marlênio, who traveled a lot. They had a little girl, Samantha, who played with her employer's daughter.

What was Samantha like?

Samantha was great. She wasn't stuck-up. Teresa didn't like stuck-up people. Stuck-up people don't make it with me, she said. Too bad they moved. It was real sudden. I helped them pack for the move.

Where'd they move to?

Cuiabá.

Was it them who told you that?

No. It was Nice, the maid.

Teresa went on to say that they'd been nervous lately. Something had happened, she didn't know what, something bad, that made Dona Érica very nervous. She cried a lot. They hired a security guard to take care of the girl. They were afraid of kidnapping.

About the church, Teresa didn't know much. She had gone to a few services but didn't like them. The evangelicals were forbidden to cut their hair, dance, or go to the movies. Teresa didn't care about the movies, but she liked to cut her hair. I don't think God has anything to do with that. With hair. If he were against us cutting our hair, he would have invented hair that didn't grow, that was Teresa's theory. I think the evangelicals go overboard, she said. I like a normal church better. I go when I want to, do what I want to, pray when I want to, it's easier. Even though it doesn't work, they say. The evangelicals. Nice says, Teresa continued, that she has a better life than I do, she gets paid more, better clothes, her father doesn't drink, 'cause her church is better than mine. That could be. Dona Érica says that when they open a church somewhere, in the same place a hospital shuts down. I don't know if the hospital here closed down.

After dinner, I took Teresa home. A really nice girl, I thought. Honest. She would be willing to go back to the hotel with me, but I can't go to bed with a woman with sweaty hands.

The night was cool, I parked the car two blocks from the hotel and walked back. I decided to leave for Cuiabá the next morning. Anderson was too slow, I thought.

The clerk at the reception desk handed me the key. A man was here looking for you, he said. He didn't know anything more. Must have been Anderson. Two, actually, the receptionist went on. They didn't leave a message.

I took the first blow to the head when I put the key in the lock to my room. Quick, I heard somebody say. I couldn't see who was talking, then I was struck again and everything went black.

I don't know how much time passed. When I woke up, I was on the floor in the room, and someone was kicking me in the stomach and the back.

Still wanna talk to Marlênio, you bastard? one of the guys asked. My head was throbbing. What do you want with Marlênio? Answer, you fucker.

More kicks. I saw the sneaker of one of them. Along with the pain came anxiety. I vomited. I tasted blood in my mouth.

Look, the guy said, he wants to say something. What do you wanna say, you son of a bitch?

While they kicked me in the head, the chest, the back, kicked as hard as they could, I remembered Marlênio, on the videotapes that Jonas gave me. You despair, Marlênio was saying, you become irritated, but what you must do at those times is to call out to the Lord, the Holy Spirit, come unto me, anoint me with Thy grace. I started laughing, they went on kicking.

Talk, you fucker, said the guy who was kicking me. What are you laughing at?

The blows came from all sides. I'm a servant of God, said a woman that Marlênio introduced as a witness to God's miracle. I came to know the hand of the Lord after I bought the Warrior of Victory card. I was ironing, and I saw Bishop Érica on television talking about the Warrior of Victory card. I bought the card because of my daughter, who was out of work, and the very next day they called my daughter and today she's working. Shouts, crying. More punches and kicks. Blood. In my house everybody bought the card. My daughter's boyfriend bought a card too, and now another miracle came to us, a brand-new car. Brand-new, repeated Marlênio in his elegant suit, brand-new, servant of God.

We're gonna break your arm if you don't talk, you fool.

God has wrought many miracles through Warrior of Victory cards. That's the last thing I remember, I started laughing nonstop and said I wanted to buy God's card, the miracle comes with the card, I said, laughing. That was when they kicked me in the head and everything went black.

I woke up in the back seat of my car, with my right arm in a cast.

Everything hurt, my bones, my face, my head.

Máiquel, are you awake?

It was Anderson.

You really took a beating, he said.

I couldn't keep my eyes open. I wanted to take a look in the mirror. I had the sensation of my head being three times its size.

Where's Tiger? I asked. My mouth, my tongue, everything ached.

Here, he said, beside me. I'm taking you somewhere safe. Did you see who did this?

Marlênio's people, I said.

How many were there?

I didn't know.

Anderson said he had some informants in the police. Somebody ratted you out this morning. The Campo Grande police were going to arrest you tonight. It was all set up, it'd be a field day. The media had already been informed of the operation. You were going to be the lead story. They even knew what hotel you were staying at. Marlênio went the whole nine yards. If it wasn't him, then you've got lots of enemies, because someone went to the precinct and gave them the address of your hotel, along with your record.

I phoned to warn you, Anderson continued. The guy at the desk said you were in your room. But you didn't answer. I found that strange. When I got to the hotel you were unconscious.

I tried to sit up. My head was heavy. Spinning.

I think it's better for you to lie down, he said. It'll take some time for us to get there.

I want to go to Cuiabá, I said. Érica's there.

She was, Anderson said. By now she must be on her way to Roraima. The plan is Boa Vista. A church for Indians. I found that out.

We traveled all night. I thought about asking why he was helping me, but I began to feel a cold sweat, my head was throbbing. Our problem here, I heard Santana say, his mouth bleeding, the words falling onto me, our problem, he went on saying, our problem is that we don't have bullfighting. So they're always wanting to beat up on someone. And it has nothing to do with justice or morality, it has to do with beating people up, I woke up, kicks, they were kicking me in the stomach, the head, the car was jolting, Marlênio's sending a message: an eye for an eye, a tooth for a tooth, you fucker. The sweat dripped from my forehead. I fainted.

We're there, said Anderson. Morning had already broken.

I saw a sea of black canvas tents when I got out of the car. It's a camp for the landless, Anderson explained. You'll be safe here, he said. We're near Rondonópolis.

Anderson held me up. It's just to that tent over there, he said, let's go, take a deep breath. My clothes were covered in blood.

Now I was on a mat, inside a tent, and my arm was in a cast. My shirt smelled of vomit. I couldn't open my eyes completely, my face was too swollen.

He's the camp coordinator, Anderson said, pointing to an old man who was looking at me with curiosity. You fainted, Máiquel. I found a doctor in the city. You'll have to put up with the cast for a time.

After the old man left us to ourselves, Anderson explained that the advantage of that place was that the police didn't go there. This is federal land, he said. Naturally we're paying for the lodging. I've done this before.

Anderson showed me a local newspaper. It wasn't till yesterday that I found out you're famous. And now they're dredging it all up again.

My picture was there. *Outlaw Sought* was the headline. It was a repeat of the story from São Paulo, only with a bigger spread. I wasn't about to waste my time reading it.

You know what it would mean for a hick cop from here to nab you? Shit, it's like winning the lottery. You'd better hide out in the woods, find some other road, he said. The guys in Campo Grande said they're going to find you regardless.

What about Tiger? I asked.

Over there, he said, pointing off to the side. He sleeps more than you do.

I asked why he was doing this for me.

Not for you, he said. For Jonas. I love Jonas.

I later found out it had nothing to do with Jonas, but with Jonas's wife. More specifically, with her pussy. That's the simple truth. Anderson was having an affair with Heloísa, Jonas's wife. He told me. Not just like that, spelled out, because Anderson's no fool. But he told me. He told me by not telling.

I overheard him talking on his cellphone to Jonas. Keep calm, he said a thousand times. I felt like I was Jonas's son. He's safe now, Anderson told Jonas, who mustn't have understood a thing. Fuck it, he was probably thinking. Jonas didn't give a shit about my safety. How's Heloísa? Anderson asked. Tell her I said hello.

Heloísa, the bitch, called back right away. Your husband was happy, Anderson told her, I gave his client the VIP treatment. He spoke softly, whispering, he thought I was groggy, unconscious, there on the mat. But my hearing is like an ear trumpet.

Heloísa was a whore. Women, I had learned, are no good. They can only be faithful for two years. Then they start putting out for everybody. A sideways glance, looking for another sucker.

Call me tonight, sweetheart, he said. I love you. You're luscious. I'm going to fuck your brains out.

And that's how I got the VIP treatment. I became something special for Anderson. Me and my problems, how about that.

Of course I had to shell out a pile of dough. And in all the confusion a large part of my money vanished. I had to pay everybody and his brother, Anderson said. Fuck it, I thought. As long as I stayed free and made it to Roraima.

Your car's stored here, he said. But I think you should change the plates, or better yet get rid of it.

I felt weak. I had lots of things to do. Run away. Get revenge. Catch those sons of bitches. I wanted to get up and get out of there. But instead I turned over on my side and stayed there, thinking bad thoughts, feeling pain and letting time go by.

IO

An ugly, foggy day. This here, said Ana, looking at the black canvas of the tents, the gray sky, looks like a photo in the newspaper. All black-and-white. I had seen worse. But it's ours, she said. We took it, by force, she said proudly.

The day after my arrival, Ana came to visit me, hair down to her waist, shorts, a plate of beans in her hands. You moaned all night long, she said. Why'd they do that to you?

I liked Ana, she was neither ugly nor pretty, squatting beside me, nice legs, I told her that, not that day, later, when she invited me to go for a walk with her.

The tents were crowded up against one another, like in a shanty town, and every dawn there was a general hubbub. That's how I met Ana and her mother Zoraide. How close they were. They were always babbling like a couple of magpies. Ana, go get some water from the well. She farted, the old woman. Prrrrrrrrrrr. She was like Tiger. And she coughed, because she smoked a lot. She'd hawk. Rssssssss. There's blood in my spit, she said. I'm going to die. Prrrrrrrrrrr.

The first few days, in pain, I didn't move, listening to the noise and picturing the confusion. When it rained, the canvas didn't stop anything; everything turned into a sea of mud. The ones who were really fucked were the children. Three of them died while I was there. At night, the people would get together and talk about the subject, occupy, resist, produce, they couldn't agree, it seemed. They would talk about taking over new land, and I didn't really understand.

To tell the truth, what with the rain, my aches, the heat under the canvas, I just closed my eyes and everything melted into a nightmare, the beating, sleep, the noise.

I felt woozy. Every tent offered a piece of conversation to muddle my brain. They raided the kitchen again, they said. They stole manioc from the field. Later, I learned there was a shanty town not far from the camp.

I'm gonna put a bullet in those sons of bitches, someone said. I kill myself sweating in the sun, and that cripple comes and steals? Planting, they don't plant.

There's a man who comes here to smoke marijuana, complained a woman. Later I understood that the woman didn't care about the marijuana; the problem was that the man was collecting anything plastic in the camp. The plastic is ours. Cans, paper, all the garbage is ours, she said. We can sell it.

There was a lot of talking going on, but what I paid attention to was the conversation between Ana and her mother. That boy, he needs to get out of bed, the old lady said. He needs to eat. What do you suppose he did wrong, Ana?

With Ana's visits I got to know the history of the camp. They had been there for three years. There were two hundred and eighty families, and they planted beans, manioc, corn, rice, nothing that worked out, because everything dried up, parched, flooded, wilted, real shitty. No tractor, no seeds. Nothing but muscle power, said Ana. Right at the start, a judge had ruled the camp could stay there for thirty days. After the deadline, the police invaded, busting heads, and they made a new request for more time, the request was denied, a hell of a brawl, and the camp was still there. Without producing enough. As bad as before. Or worse. They dug a well. Ana took care of the school and the kids. Her father, a leader of the landless movement, had been murdered by a bullet in the face.

Let's go, Ana said, let's go for a walk, she said that morning.

Since the beating, I couldn't be on my feet for more than ten minutes. Everything hurt.

We walked around the camp. Ana told me that before the occupation junk of every kind was tossed there, plastic, shoes, old tires, bottles, cans, animal carcasses, car chassies; they even claim, she said, that it was a place for dumping bodies, police and drug dealers would throw the corpses here.

She had pretty hands. Small. Delicate. I started to find Ana prettier by the day. And me all fucked up, with Tiger lame, dragging behind me. She had a lot of things to say, and me with my head empty. I felt stupid compared to Ana. Silly. Actually, the only thing that came to mind was the crap I'd found in Érica's house about the evangelical churches. Ana wouldn't want to know about that subject.

We went to the collective kitchen and there we ran into Osório, having coffee.

This is Máiquel, Ana said.

I saw right away that the guy hated me.

That's just his way, Ana said. Don't pay any attention.

There was something going on between the two of them.

It's over, she told me later, after Osório left. He's very jealous, too chauvinist for my taste. He wants to keep women in the kitchen, and that's not me.

Is he the boss? I asked.

We don't have a boss in the camp, Ana explained. No sheriff, no owner, no director, no president. Just a coordinator. Here things work from the bottom up.

I didn't understand, but I didn't ask for an explanation.

They all talked too much, not only Ana, everybody. A lot of blather. It even made me sleepy. What's important for us is the nucleus, the family, they would say. Hearing that, you'd think everything there was wonderful, but if you took a close look you saw it was crap, the mud, all the poverty.

That night, I went with Ana to an assembly; that's what they called the quarrels they had almost every night. You'll like it, she said. I went because I wanted to stay close to her. But it was a real drag.

The one shouting the most was Osório, who didn't take his eyes off Ana. Or me. They promised us food, Osório said, so we wouldn't invade other lands. But we don't want rice or beans. Or agreements.

Ana was sitting on the ground, in Bermudas, her legs crossed. I was dying to get out of there with her.

From time to time Ana would look at me and smile. Do you understand? she asked.

I wasn't paying much attention. I mean, I was just paying attention to her legs.

We're going to go on tearing down fences. We want land. We want to stop being slaves, they said. Applause. I applauded too.

Afterward, when the meeting was over, we headed back toward my tent. There was already something good going on between us, I could feel it.

Ana explained that she was there because she believed in the movement, believed in agrarian reform. How about you? she asked.

Was I going to say I was a fugitive? Never. Me, nothing, I replied. I'm just taking time out.

She said something else about the movement, wanted to know my opinion. But what could I say? I didn't have an opinion. I detested hoes. Planting potatoes, harvesting, tilling the land, none of that was my thing.

It's good to have an ideal, she said.

Ana, shouted Osório.

We were arriving at my tent when he appeared, with a machete in his belt. We hadn't hit it off, that was very clear from the start.

We'll talk later, I said. I didn't want a confrontation.

I don't know what was said between the two of them, I only know that five minutes later we were laughing together in my tent.

The next day, wherever I went, people looked at me out of the corner of their eyes, whispering. Laughing.

They're a bunch of chauvinists, Ana said. Just because I used to be with Osório, they think I can't have a life of my own. To hell with them. I couldn't care less.

It's not quite like that, they told me later, in the kitchen. Osório had a fling with a woman in the city, and Ana is getting even. You shouldn't get involved. It's a quarrel between husband and wife. Maybe so. But I wasn't the one doing the chasing. It was Ana who came to my tent as soon as it got dark. The bad part was knowing that her mother was right next door. She would stare at me, in the kitchen, or when I went to the well for water. She must prick up her ears when we fucked.

Except for Osório, I was well liked in the camp. To tell the truth, money will make you well liked anywhere. Right away, by spreading around a few bills in the kitchen to the women who took care of the kettles of beans, I guaranteed my grub.

Besides that, the landless people liked my car. Beto, Ana's cousin, was the one who used it the most. He would go to the city with the trunk full of potatoes, manioc, and corn. I'm going to find a buyer for your car, he said.

The best thing for you would be to get rid of the car, Anderson had said. Not that the police knew about my car, but you know how it is, he said, it's best not to make things easy for them.

For Sale, I wrote on a piece of cardboard and put it in the rear window of the car. *See the driver*. But in that middle of nowhere nobody wanted to buy anything.

There's a Japanese at the municipal market who's interested, Beto said. A vegetable vendor. A fishmonger.

Later I found out that it was all bullshit. Get a fake plate if you plan to go on using it, that was the condition I stipulated. A false plate was the least precaution possible.

Before the trips to town, I liked watching the arguments among the landless; no one could agree on the price of beans, there was no way they could come to an understanding. Actually, there was. But later someone would always end up selling the produce for a lower price, claiming they didn't know about the agreement. I wasn't told, they complained. Beto himself always did that.

In the evening, I would take Tiger for a walk along the trails and paths of the camp. Other dogs would join us, mangy, starving, and compared to them Tiger looked good. At least he was only lame. Soon I learned that people from the neighboring shanty town would come over to smoke marijuana and package cocaine. Armed and everything. I liked to hang with them and shoot the breeze.

Don't you want to drop by the school with me? asked Ana, when she saw me with nothing to do.

Sometimes she would drag me to the shed where she taught the children that the rich were the ruination of Brazil. And they don't even know how to plant beans, like the song says.

Osório was always after me, jerking my chain. Once, half loaded, he tried to pick a fight. I didn't bite.

One Friday I went to the city with Beto. I'd been in the camp for almost a month. While he was negotiating at the municipal market, I decided to go for a walk.

I phoned Anderson.

What's happening, man? he asked.

Same old shit, I said. I asked if things had calmed down.

Fuck, man, it's one big shit-storm, he said. The prisoners rioted there in Rondonópolis, he said.

What prisoners?

There's a prison there in Rondonópolis, he said.

What a fuck-up, I thought, the guy brings me to a place where there's a prison.

They decapitated the hostages, it was insane. Go back to the camp and hunker down there. The highways must be swarming with cops. Yesterday they tried to kill the warden. The situation looks bad. There's police everywhere.

What about me? I asked.

Beats me, he said. They mustn't be thinking about you, but if you're caught, tough luck.

I asked what was the best way to make it to Roraima.

In this situation, he said, the best thing is not to go to Roraima.

It didn't even enter my mind not to go after Érica and Marlênio. Fuck me if I'd leave them alone.

In that case, he said, go up. Take the north route and hightail it. Head for the forest, the jungle. Follow the goat-trails and who's gonna find you?

Anderson went crazy when I told him I still hadn't sold the car.

That's stupid, man. It leaves a trail. Be careful.

I hung up, dying to get back to the camp. They decapitated hostages. What crap. Beto would pick me up at 5.30 in a square nearby. I decided to kill some time by getting a beer at the bar. What shit, rioting. I ordered another beer. It leaves a trail, Anderson said. The car.

You need to come here at the time of the meeting, said a guy to his friend, at the next table. There's a kind of backwards race, you know?

I couldn't manage to tune out the conversation. A couple of jerks.

The one who comes in last wins, understand? There's a thousand events, autocross, tug-of-war, it's a competition of bikes from the Center-West, understand? Wrestling in gelatin, understand? Real cool.

Those two guys there with beards, drinking and talking stupidities. Fag stuff, I thought.

I decided not to wait for Beto.

I got a bus to the city limits and then walked a long way. It was 8.15 when I reached the camp. Before going to my tent, I stopped by the well. I couldn't take that cast anymore.

I was there, removing the gauze, when Osório showed up. We're organizing a demonstration, he said, for two days from now.

My arm, without the cast, felt like a feather.

You could help, he said. We're working with you; one hand washes the other.

I said I'd think about it. I couldn't even feel my hand. I mean, nothing but pain.

It's a show of force against the murderous landowners of the region here, Osório continued. They killed one of our comrades three months ago. Did you know that this place, which today is our farmland, used to be a secret cemetery for those corrupt landowners?

I said I'd think about it.

Think about what? he asked. What've you got to lose?

I wasn't about to say that I'm a fugitive. But he did it for me.

Look here, Máiquel, you're in deep shit, I know that, man. You're running from the police, and we're helping you. I know Anderson, he said. I'm the one who saved your ass.

I don't like threats. If that's how it is, I said, I'm out of here.

I turned my back, and before I'd taken two steps, the guy came after me at full blast.

Listen here, he said, grabbing my shirt.

I turned and saw that Osório had a knife in his hand.

Everything happened very fast. Suddenly, the knife was in my hand.

I don't know if I killed Osório. I only know that he stayed there, on the ground, blood gushing from his belly.

11

Fools are never bored was written on the bumper of the tractor-trailer in front of us. That barge, said Josias, carries almost an entire harvest of soy.

It wasn't until then that I realized Josias wasn't mute. He had a tongue, Josias.

Fifty-four tons, he continued. That's why the price of hauling keeps going down. And it makes us crawl along like turtles, you know?

Later, I understood what had happened. Josias took an upper to stay awake. That's when he started talking like mad and spent the rest of the stretch chattering away. He'd say something, all the time checking the dashboard to see if his tire pressure was okay, and say, Tires okay, oil okay, brakes okay, as if I got any of it. I love this life, he said. Love the highway. I especially love going home. He once worked between four walls, Josias, but it wasn't for him. His head couldn't take it. He was hired and sent packing a week later. In an office, my brain shorts out, he said. It doesn't work. If you want to see my ideas blossom, just let me free to roam. Once I hit the road, I never wanted any other life. I'm gonna buy one of those rigs, Josias said, excited. Just like the one in front of us. Or even bigger. As soon as things get better. And they are getting better. I'm sick of being honest, he said, laughing. Now I have my schemes, like everybody else. Here in Brazil, if you want to get ahead in life, you've gotta steal, you've gotta be a thief. Everybody steals. Oil okay. Brakes okay.

Any news about Osório? I asked. I wanted to know if I'd killed the guy, but Josias didn't know anything.

Just fantastic schemes to make money. The pill made him talk my ears off about cargos of stolen lumber, offloading trucks, transporting acetone to the cartels in Bolivia, rival gangs that attack each other on the road, that was the future, he said, lots of money, real money, that's the only way to make money. All you have to do is drive and take your cut. I don't steal, believe me. I just drive. It's the others who steal. They steal and I drive. I don't steal and I don't kill. The problem is safety. There's a stretch of this road that's pure danger. I don't work with acetone. I've got a little boy. I've told them, I'll haul any stolen cargo, lumber, tires, trucks, but never acetone, I'm no fool. It leads to shit, he said.

Our truck used to be full of lumber, Josias said, you know, we're selling off the Amazon, I go up and down this country, and all I see is soy. Soy and more soy. And burned-over land. Apuí, Lábrea, Manicoré, Boca do Acre, Novo Aripuanã, you used to arrive there and find pure forest, I mean, you couldn't even get there, today you can, and there's nothing but land-clearing. It's all pasture, grain, timber, that's all there is. Fuck the rainforest, that's our politicians' policy. In Lábrea, in the south of Amazonas, the guys killed themselves to do away with the forest before the environmental protection agency got there. That's what happened around there. And today, for example, here I am, packed to the gills with mahogany. But sometimes I haul *ipê* wood. And I also take dismantled trucks, or else drive the rig to Paraguay. I go to Bolivia, and everything is cool, just like the doctor ordered, with the chassis altered, new plates, everything just the way it should be, brand-new and legal.

DON'T DRINK WATER, FISH SCREW IN IT read the bumper of the truck that passed us. I had one advantage, when I wanted to I could stop listening. Josias went on talking, talking, talking, but I stopped hearing him. I closed my eyes and thought about Ana, her face when I was stuffing my things into my backpack.

I'm going with you, she said.

I was in a hurry, woozy, anxious to get out of there, and Ana came with that business. Then get ready, I said, I'll come for you in an hour.

Beto, Ana's cousin, was waiting for me on the dirt road leading to the camp, when I arrived with Tiger and the backpack. What happened? he asked.

I fucked up, I said, getting into the car. I need to get away. It started to rain. I need to get away right now, I said. I told him about Osório. They're going to find his body soon, I said.

We didn't say anything for a time.

Beto thought it was funny when I asked if he didn't want to buy my car. What with? We stared at the rain. I've got an idea, he said after a time. Somebody from the movement. Got a few deals going. Transports hot cargo of timber. That's the way Beto talked. Half-sentences. My part of the deal, he said, would be the car.

I went for the idea in a heartbeat.

We went to a gas station.

I'm gonna use the telephone, Beto said. Wait here for me.

Everything's set, he said when he returned.

Then we drove for a long time until we found a cement factory near the Rondonópolis exit.

You can get out, he said.

How do I know everything's okay? I asked.

You don't, he answered, just my word. A guy's coming to pick you up. He can be trusted. He'll take you to Cuiabá. His name's Josias. You can trust him.

I waited in the rain for over an hour, till a guy in a dilapidated minivan showed up.

I'm a friend of Josias's, he said.

We spent the night at a farm. I slept in a tent.

I didn't understand what their game was, who was in charge, or what the people of the landless movement had to do with any of it. They worked all night, sawing and stacking timber.

Less than twenty-four hours later I was on the road, headed for Cuiabá.

The only bad part was leaving Ana in the lurch. I could've said goodbye, sent her a note, whatever, anything but disappear like that.

The noise from the motor made me sleepy. Tiger was quiet, with his head in my lap. I fell asleep with Josias talking about getting rich.

It was midnight when I woke up with Josias nudging me. Police, he said. Stay in the truck and keep your mouth shut. Let me handle everything.

We parked by the side of the road, obeying the cops' gestures, and Josias got out, ready to cooperate.

The plan really did work. Before I could locate my false papers in the backpack, he'd already returned. Everything's OK, he said, we're good to go. My expression must've been awful. You're scared of the wrong guys, he said, the danger is from criminals, the traffickers. What we gotta be afraid of is the thieves who want our cargo. The police are our partners. They're our friends, they work for us, serve as our escort. That's what you paid for. Didn't you trade a car to get to Cuiabá? It's like pizza. Fast delivery.

But first, he said, we're going to make a quick stop in Chapada dos Guimarães. I've got some business to take care of there, it's fast, and in two hours we'll be on our way.

As soon as we entered the city, Josias parked at a gas station. I'll be back in just a little while, he said.

It was a woman, that was for sure. He even put on deodorant before getting out.

I stretched my legs and went back to sleep. I woke up at ten in the morning with the sun in my face and a buzzard on the truck's hood. I didn't like it. It sucks to wake up and see a buzzard staring you in the face.

I got out of the truck, and Josias soon appeared, carrying a cup of coffee. I'm all messed up, he said. But we're within the deadline, in fact we're ahead of time, he said, offering me the coffee. We'll leave here in late afternoon. I'm gonna wander around, he continued. This place is as close to heaven as you'll ever find.

I strolled around with Tiger, looking at the city. Chapada was pretty, I'd never seen houses like that. The highest part of the roofs wasn't in the middle of the houses but in front, and the tiles were clay. I thought about calling Eunice and telling her that. This city, Eunice, is different from the rest, I'd say. It's not just fences and flat roofs. Or tar roofs. Or aluminum windows. Eunice would like it here. Not even all the bricks were alike. They weren't concrete blocks. They were something else. I liked that. The church was a real beauty.

The first thing I did was stop at a news-stand and buy the local paper. I wanted to see if it mentioned me. Whether Osório had died. But it only talked about the rebellion in the Rondonópolis prison, the inmates who had decapitated the hostages, and other barbarities.

The news that made my jaw drop was beside the photo of a pretty girl, who could very well have been Miss Cuiabá but was the woman who had swiped all the money in my wallet the night we spent together in Campo Grande. Sílvia, the bitch. MATO GROSSO BEAUTY KILLS FATHER AND GODFATHER read the headline. I knew the story. The paper didn't say why she'd done it. Stabbed him nineteen times. Her father, she shot while he was sleeping. She was a fugitive. Sílvia had realized her dream. She was quick, I thought. I don't doubt she used the money she stole from me to buy the gun. Shit. To think that I slept with the woman. And Osório must be alive; at least there was no mention of him.

I wandered around the city all morning. I bought a red collar for Tiger. At lunchtime, I was near a square when I saw a woman taking the spare tire out of her trunk. I went over to her.

I'm awful at this, she said, can you give me a hand?

I changed the tire for her.

I'm going to get it fixed later, she said. Thank you very much, you're very kind. Where are you staying?

Her name was Cecilia, and she owned an inn. Wouldn't you like to have lunch there?

When we awake, I want to tell you how happiness is gonna cascade over people. I liked the music they were playing in the restaurant. Tom Zé, she said.

I came here, she said, while I ate a dish of rice and butternut, because of the region's electromagnetic flux.

It's gonna cascade over people, it's gonna cascade over people, it's gonna.

We have here the Bivac corridor, have you heard of it? It's a channel of energy that makes it possible for the initiates to have direct contact with intergalactic beings.

Girl, happiness is the greatest thing, it's full of life, it's full of moths, said the music. Funny, I thought, to speak of happiness that way.

Over Chapada, Cecilia continued, there's a hole through which cosmic energy enters that doesn't come from any part of the planet.

I didn't understand a damn thing. *It's full of year, it's full of cheer, it's full of beer.* I liked the song.

The food was very good. No pesticides, she said.

Cecilia must have been close to fifty, and I think she was interested in me. She asked if I'd like to see the area.

As we began climbing the mountain, she put the car in neutral. Look at this, she said. The car continued on its way up. Magnetic forces can do anything, she said mysteriously. It wasn't till then that I realized she really was an old lady. She had the typical old lady's way of widening her eyes. The car's climbing, she said, and it's not in gear. Isn't that fantastic? I once saw a flying saucer here, did you know that?

All this was once covered in ice, Cecilia went on excitedly. That was millions of years ago. Then the ice melted, it became a sea, then everything dried up, grass grew, the dinosaurs came, I don't know if in that order, because she spoke very fast and I was getting confused. A short time ago Chapada came about, which is this lovely thing, said Cecilia, these sandstone mountains that I never tire of seeing. I didn't believe in God till I came to Chapada, but when I arrived here, after a failed marriage, destroyed, totally destroyed, by alcohol, after losing the custody of my children because of that son of a bitch my ex-husband, I saw this place and something changed in my soul. I concluded that, if this wonder exists, if Chapada dos Guimarães exists,

God exists. Look at those mountains, she said, doesn't it get to you?

When we arrived at the Aroe Jari cavern, Cecilia and I were walking hand in hand.

This is the place that gave me peace, she said. It was here that I found the peace to stop drinking. And I was drinking a bottle of whiskey a day. And gin, I loved gin. At eleven in the morning I would start with my little gin. Did you know this cavern was a shelter for primates and Indians of the Bororo and Caipó tribes?

The grotto was enormous. There's room for a samba school here, Cecilia said when we went in.

Afterward, Cecilia rolled a joint and we smoked. She continued on her kick, saying that God was everything. God was intelligence. He was stone. The wind.

Do you believe in God? she asked.

No, I answered.

Cecilia took another drag, holding the smoke in her lungs. But what about Chapada?

What about it?

Isn't Chapada proof of God?

Beats me.

Spend a week here and you'll start to believe in God. I guarantee it. What's that tattooed on your arm?

I rolled up my sleeve and showed her the entire tattoo.

Fuck you, she read. My husband was like that too. You know? she said, that energy you carry around isn't good for you. I can feel it now that we're closer. It's the type of energy that weighs you down.

I didn't say anything.

God exists, Cecilia said. And this place is proof of it.

The marijuana must have gotten Tiger stoned, because he started trying to bite his tail.

You should look for a tattoo artist and do something about that tattoo, write: *I wouldn't try to fuck you*. That would attract positive things to you. Good attracts good. The problem with having a *Fuck you* like that is, I don't know, it works in the long run, you understand? From saying it so much, you end up actually fucking yourself. It's like a prayer, as if you wanted to fuck yourself. You repeat Fuck you, Fuck you, Fuck you, and then things really do fuck up. Aren't you going to say anything?

What did she want me to say? Fuck it.

You know, she said after a time, the reason you see everything blue on the horizon? It's the concentration of oxygen. Lots of oxygen. That's why the Earth is blue.

I still didn't say anything. A woman stoned on weed is a handful. And I didn't like smoking marijuana. It makes you sleepy. And hungry. Cecilia was right. You end up turning on the Fuck you when you smoke marijuana. I mean, I don't know if that's exactly what she was saying. I wasn't paying much attention. All I saw was Tiger limping back and forth. Happiness cascaded down on Tiger.

On the way back to the city, Cecilia didn't say anything. She left me in the square.

Thanks for the tire, she said.

Same to you, I thought about answering. But she was the type who had no sense of humor. A bore, Cecilia.

I wouldn't try to fuck you, what a laugh. I went back to the gas station, waited a long time, eating all kinds of crap I bought in a nearby bar.

Josias didn't show up till ten that night, all wrinkled, looking like he'd gone I don't know how long without sleeping.

He took a couple more uppers and we left for Cuiabá.

12

I'm in Nova Iguaçu, I thought when I opened my eyes, in Eunice's bedroom, bumbum paticundum prurugundum, the sound was coming from outside, I woke up to the beat, saw the television on, the window to the right, the dresser to the left, and suddenly what had been happening the last few days happened again, Eunice's bedroom transformed into a hotel room. Cuiabá, I remembered. I'm in Cuiabá.

It was all very fast, there wasn't even time to count to five, I opened my eyes and in my dizziness didn't know where I was. One day I thought I was married to Érica, that I was in our house in São Bernardo, another day that I was at the camp with Ana, a different sensation every day, a place, a time, it wasn't good.

It was funny that now I didn't dream about Érica anymore. Not that way. I'd lost the ability. In the period when I was hiding out at Santana's country place, without anything to do, with no place to go, running from the police, I developed a special technique to dream about Érica, and I liked it. I would close my eyes and she would just come. She'd enter my head, and I didn't even need to go to sleep. And if I did go to sleep, she'd stay there.

She'd ask me to take her back. She'd say, I love you, Máiquel. I want to come back.

Come back, I would say. I wasn't angry at Érica. No pain.

Let's dance, Máiquel. Relax your hips. Relax your arms. She said a lot of things, Érica, she laughed, you know? Máiquel, the difference between us is that you're very stiff.

It was true, I was stiff. Érica would say whatever came into her head, but even for that, for talking, I was stiff. My face sometimes turned to stone. The words wouldn't come out. I kept silent.

Say something, Máiquel.

I still love you, Érica. That I did manage to say, sometimes.

There were also other ways that Érica would come to me. It could be an ad in the newspaper, for example, *Sun Place Hills, a hundred and thirty square meters of private area, four bedrooms, financing available.* Did you see this, Máiquel? Why don't we buy it? Exclusive offers. At times like that, shit, I could feel my heart beating everywhere, I didn't have the desire to do anything else, I just wanted to close my eyes and see Érica dancing around in my head. Buy an apartment. Build something. Of our own. Pay in installments. That's what I liked. Her plans. For the next few years, I went on dreaming. Less and less, 'cause that's how people work; you dream less and less the older you get, the fewer things you have to dream about. And you forget too. You dry up, rot.

Now, my technique didn't work anymore. I mean, it did work. The dream would start out just the way it should. Érica would appear, not skinny like she was when we met, chewing on gum, but pumped up, like in the photos Jonas got me, in heels, playing the lady, asking, Why do you think I left, Máiquel? But the one who answered, Because you killed Cledir, was Eunice. Murderer. Or Cledir herself. Or some other woman whose name I didn't know. Real confusion, the dream. And I wasn't even sleeping. I dreamed with my eyes open.

And what did you do when I left? they asked, the Éricas. You loitered around, they said, hesitating like some clown, wasting time, and us hoping, Samantha and me, you'd do just that, you'd come after us, they said. Hands on her hips. Fingers pointed at my nose. That you'd turn yourself in to the police. But you ran away, Máiquel. You hid out, wherever, in rotten holes. Living the disgusting life of a fugitive. What are you today? A fugitive. Nothing more. Years and years of living like an animal, without so much as a phone call to your own daughter. You're a shitty father, Máiquel. A shitty husband. You don't even know how to apologize. Or pay for your sins.

I couldn't take anymore of those women rattling my cage even in dreams. A nightmare, the dreams. So I stopped dreaming.

But that day I woke up in Cuiabá. In the square across the street there was a store that sold CDs, and starting in early morning they would put on loud music.

I gave up complaining, the owner of the boarding house said. They don't give a damn if I show up.

Everybody here likes it, that's what the store owner told me when I went to complain, at the boarding-house owner's suggestion. And what can I do for you?

I ended up buying a Zeca Pagodinho CD. And I didn't ask him to lower the volume of the music. It wasn't so bad to wake up to music. A jackhammer would be a lot worse. Or some corn-fritter vendor.

Remember not to eat that fish they call *pacu*, Anderson said when I called him the day before. If you eat *pacu* you'll never leave the city, the legend says. Or are you planning to settle down there?

Very funny, I replied.

I had called Anderson early in the morning to find out several things, one, if Osório had died.

You stick a knife in the guy's belly and then call me to find out if he died? Usually they die, said Anderson, they die quicker if you put a bullet in their mug, but knives usually do the job. And you fucked me with that, man. They got mad as shit at me, the landless. Because of you. And they told me they're not gonna hide anybody at the camp anymore. Something else: Osório wanted to lodge a complaint against you. The only reason he didn't was because he took the car from Beto that you left as payment. He slapped Beto around a bit and that was that.

Fuck it, I thought. At least he was alive. I was glad to hear that. What about Ana? I asked.

You take me for the gossip columnist for the landless of Rondonópolis? Anderson said. I don't even know who Ana is. Now get a pen and write this down. He gave me the information about his account. If you want me to go on working for you, make a deposit in my account, you know how much, do it and call me tomorrow with a list of what you want.

I did what he said. First I had to open my backpack and count what remained of my dough. A thick wad, the money. Two thousand eight hundred and thirty, after the deposit for Anderson. I didn't have to worry, at least not for a while.

I had been in Cuiabá for almost two days. During the trip, I asked Josias if he could arrange a ride for me to the north of the country.

To where?

Anywhere, I said. North. I need to get to Boa Vista. Using your scheme, I continued.

Paying, we can set up anything, he said.

That's the problem, I said, I don't want to pay, I want to get paid. I know how to drive.

On the way, Josias had told me a lot of stories. About how you made money taking acetone and ether to San Matías, in Bolivia. A huge market, he said. I might even make a profit. Steal a truck. It could work out fine.

Give me some time, Josias said. I'm gonna think about it and get back to you soon.

That morning, I didn't even consider getting out of bed. The heat was stifling. I called Anderson again, to check if he had news of Érica.

I'm a detective, not a magician. Sit your ass down and let me work. Take advantage of the city. Did you know that

Cuiabá has women all over the place? There's more than twelve thousand extra women in the city. That's what the census says.

I hung up and decided to bathe Tiger, who was stinking up the room with his wet-carpet smell.

At times I had the impression he was going to talk. You don't fool me, you fart-bucket. I know you're not a dog. You're an old hippie. You did so much acid that you turned into a dog. Now you don't know how to turn back into a man.

What's the problem, dog? Must be the collar.

I took the collar off Tiger. To tell the truth, collars don't work. Even less on an old hippie.

Eunice, I said, it's me, Máiquel. I was at a pay phone on Avenida Rio Branco.

Hi, she said, where are you? For the first time, Eunice sounded happy on the phone.

In Cuiabá, I answered.

Ah, is it cool there?

It's hot, I said. Know how they say okay here? Gasser. People in Cuiabá are funny, I said.

Did you find your daughter? Eunice asked.

Not yet. But I'm on the right track.

How nice, she said, I'm rooting for you.

Silence.

I miss you, I said.

I'm getting married, she replied. To a super cool guy. He works at the supermarket. He's the manager.

Shit, what a blow.

Máiquel? Can you hear me?

Yes, Eunice.

Are you angry?

No, I replied. Gasser.

What did you say?

Gasser, I repeated, that's okay here in Cuiabá.

I thought you'd be sad, she said. How stupid of me. You never cared about me. In fact, you never cared about anyone.

We remained silent, I didn't know what to say. Gasser, I thought about saying again.

Do you want to give me a wedding present, Máiquel? she asked. Then forget I exist. Disappear from my life.

I hung up and walked away, under a blazing sun. Eunice didn't need to treat me like that. I liked her. A supermarket manager, shit. Big fucking deal. A preacher. I walked with Tiger down the avenue, looking for a place to eat. I wasn't even hungry, what I wanted was somewhere to get away from that sun.

Pacu steak, *furrundu*, I had to ask the waitress to translate those names.

It's a dessert, she said, citron candy. Try the *surubim*, that's stewed fish with manioc, it's very good.

She was very pretty, the girl; she stood there looking at me while I gave hunks of fish to Tiger, but I was too tired to strike up a conversation. Later, they end up marrying the manager.

When I returned to the boarding house, there was a message to call Anderson. He told me he'd put listening devices in the Powerful Heart of Jesus church in Campo Grande. Good news, he said. The hotel where Érica stayed in Cuiabá was the Royal. But that doesn't matter. Forget the Royal. What you need to know is that she and Marlênio are going to Bolivia, La Paz. Go to Corumbá, he said, and take the Train of Death. That way you can kill two birds with one stone. You leave Brazilian jurisdiction, nobody can catch you, and you pick up their trail. They're still talking about that cop's death here. The best thing is for you to disappear.

But what about Roraima? Did they change their plans?

Don't know. All I know is they're scared shitless of you. Because of the girl.

Anderson told me that while I was in Campo Grande, Marlênio's people were on my tail. The big news, he said, is that Samantha knows about you, in some form. From what I understood, Érica had to explain to her the reason they were leaving the city. On the recording, she says: She's all right now, she understood that the best thing was for us to leave.

Who said that?

Érica, replied Anderson. To one of the church bishops.

But hadn't you already put taps on the church's telephones?

Not on these lines. It's a new thing. Maybe Samantha knows something. That's what I understood.

About me?

Yeah. From the conversations, I understood that maybe she knows she's registered under Marlênio's name but isn't his daughter.

The news increased my desire to kill that bastard.

Can I hear the tapes?

Go to Corumbá. I'll send the materials there. Do the following: when you get to the city, look up Nei. He'll give you the information that we're gathering about Érica.

Who's Nei? I asked.

Nei is Nei, for Chrissake. Rua Quinze de Novembro, number 600.

I wrote it down. Before hanging up, I thought about asking if Anderson knew anybody interested in a shipment of acetone. A waste of time. First, arranging to get the acetone. Going to Cáceres. Coming back. It was a lot of money, but who could say if I'd be able to put the scheme together? And I was dying to kill Marlênio.

I went to sleep with my mind made up. The next day, very early, I would leave.

13

This truck's a real workhorse, said the driver who gave me a ride to Corumbá. A workhorse, this truck. And he didn't say anything more. He was embarrassed for me. And me for him.

It was in Cuiabá itself, in the office of Josias's dispatcher, that I arranged the ride. I showed up there very early with my backpack, and with Josias's help it wasn't hard.

While I was waiting for the ride, after everything was set up, I saw the driver get a royal chewing out. How could you fuck up like that? The driver stood there, sweating, trying to explain, and the dispatcher calling him stupid, incompetent. I don't know what kind of fuck-up he'd committed.

It's bad to see someone get hauled over the coals like that.

We didn't talk again until a lot later, when we were on BR-163, on a stretch of dirt road full of potholes.

They're going to pave all of this, he said happily. Beautiful. Just imagine, the entire Amazon region paved from end to end. Oh yeah, that's going to be good. That's the only thing missing, asphalt. We've got everything else.

The truck almost got stuck in a hole the size of a Volkswagen. This thing doesn't get stuck, he said, running over an animal crossing the highway. It was an alligator, I saw. This is a workhorse, he said, it just doesn't get stuck.

Did you kill it? I said.

Yeah. Nothing you can do about those critters. They jump in front of cars, you just gotta kill them. Last week I killed a deer.

Shit, was that a drag. The guy drove badly, he had no reflexcs. He saw that I didn't like it and said that if that's how I was I'd never be able to travel in the rcgion. He'd seen everything in life. Entire families of alligators dead on the highway. And capybaras. And run over deliberately, on top of that. A bad driver would get his kicks aiming at animals. Not me, he said, I only kill by accident. You wouldn't believe what I've seen of Pantanal deer, maned wolves, spotted leopards, pumas, bush dogs, all dead on the road with their guts out. Once, he said, I saw an anteater cub on the back of its dead mother. It was enough to break your heart.

He wouldn't shut up. Now I understood why his boss had chewed him out. A boring guy, shit.

I bounced, hanging from the window, with Tiger on my lap, looking at the countryside. The rest of the trip was the same, I'd never been in those parts, my thoughts leaving me, flying off, everything I came across, every hole in the highway, capybara, bad road, good road, erosion, alligator, I slept, woke up, uneasy sleep, jabiru storks, drained, dying to arrive.

We covered over six hundred miles before we got to Corumbá. It was 7.30 in the morning when we entered the city. The first thing I did, after getting out of the truck at a gas station, was to look for Nei on rua Quinze de Novembro.

The address wasn't right, it was a butcher shop, the New World House of Meats. Off to a bad start, I thought.

I went to a pay phone at the corner and called Anderson, but he hadn't got to the office yet. I explained to his secretary what was happening.

No, you're all right, she said. Nei is Dr Anderson's cousin. He's a butcher. He's the one you should talk to.

I headed back toward the butcher shop, laughing at that 'Dr Anderson.' I wondered if Anderson had asked her to call him Doctor. Doctor was better than Mister. Mr Anderson. In my glory days I was never Dr Máiquel. I was Man of the Year. I was the Honorable. *The Santo Amaro Recreation Club has the pleasure of inviting you to its Citizen of the Year ceremony, where you will be honored for the services you have rendered to the community.* They were happy, in those days, because I had killed a lot of poor blacks. Let me introduce you to the judge, Máiquel, they said at the party. A lawyer. A pediatrician. They were all there, honoring me. Later they got angry. When I killed one of them. A white kid, a dentist's son. They were outraged. You can't kill a dentist's son, they said. I kept that invitation for a long time. I don't know why. I liked looking at it. Bunch of sons of bitches.

Assholes. It was the only thing left from all that shit. The invitation. Crumpled. Dirty.

Nei is at his country place, they told me when I arrived at the butcher shop. Come back tomorrow.

Tiger started barking at the smell of the meat.

Where's the country place? I asked.

The people at the butcher shop weren't cooperative. And I was getting irritated myself.

I explained I was there because of Anderson, who was Nei's cousin. He's expecting me, I said. I came to pick up some materials.

The guy at the counter disappeared into the rear of the shop, phoned someone and when he returned said he was going to take me to the slaughterhouse.

We left the city, and in ten minutes arrived at the place, a secret slaughterhouse. There were carcasses hanging from trees, with flies swarming around them. And Nei must've been sleeping soundly while the cows were killed with sledgehammers. He showed up wiping sleep from his face.

Máiquel, he said as he handed me the package with photos of Érica and the tapes, my cousin didn't tell me you'd be getting here today.

I felt like opening the envelope right then and there.

How long will you be here? Nei asked.

I explained that I was going to catch the Train of Death. I'm in a hurry, I said.

The first city on the Bolivian side is Puerto You should catch the train there.

131

I knew that already. I asked if he'd take me there. I'd pay, of course. My problem is the dog, I explained. Taxis and buses don't allow animals.

You should stay here in Corumbá for a day or two, Nei said, when we were on the road. These hicks like to talk. This here, he said when we passed by a large structure, this here is the replica of the obelisk built in 4,000 BC in Paris, in Concorde Square.

Shit, he was putting me to sleep. That kind of touristy talk always bored me. Three thousand years, four thousand. The names of colonels. The names of kings. War stories. I can't keep any of it in my head. I forget everything.

If you were to spend more time here, I'd take you to get to know Corumbá. The sculptures from Italy, donated by a count.

Shit, what a turn-off. I already forgot before I even saw it.

This city is too much. I wouldn't leave here for anything in the world. There's also the Pantanal Museum, he said. Do you like stuffed animals?

I like alligators, I said.

Nei left me near the Bolivian Ministry. There wasn't a soul around.

Do you know how it works? he asked.

I didn't know anything.

You'll need a visa to cross the border.

What do I have to do?

Go there with your passport and say you want a visa. Insist on it, because they drag their heels so they can catch you later Bolivia without a visa and put the bite on you.

You'd think I had a passport.

Afterward, go to that window at the side and buy your ticket.

Saying it, it seemed simple. Except everything was closed. The sun was blistering.

We said goodbye.

As I was getting out of the car, Nei asked me for a favor.

Could you take this gift to my son in Santa Cruz? he asked, showing me a colorful package.

Holy shit, I thought.

Now things were starting to fall into place.

It's a birthday present. He lives with my ex-wife.

I got out of the car, with my false documents and the package.

Before crossing the border, I opened the package. It was a miniature Scania, just like the ones in which I traveled. I broke open the wheels. Then I smashed the chassis against the ground as hard as I could. I dismantled the cab and reduced everything to pieces. Nothing. It really was a toy. I threw everything away, keeping only the boy's address, I don't know why. How was I to know the guy wasn't shitting me?

I went past the Ministry calmly. No one there to make problems for me. The real problem was buying the ticket. The window was closed, the only information there was a sign that read: *First class: twenty-five bolivianos. Second class: twenty bolivianos. Third class: fifteen bolivianos.* A shithole of a country, Bolivia.

The thing was to find a place to sleep. That's what I was going to do.

The city was ugly as sin. Dirty. I didn't like Bolivia at all. Érica was always saying she wanted to go abroad. South America, she used to say. Abroad was crap, Brazil was much better. Actually, the place resembled some of the boondocks of Brazil. Even TV there had nothing but Brazilian soap operas. The only thing that showed it was a different country was the language, which made me nervous. A bear, that language. It gets you all balled up.

A lot of noise, in the city. Lots of people too. And something I hate: those spics don't respect what Eunice called 'personal space.' Every person, Eunice said, has to have his two square meters of peace. Nobody has the right to elbow you in the street, bump into you, push their bag, their package, their suitcase, their butt, their rolls of fat, their junk against you. There ought to be a law. Very smart, Eunice was. It bothers me when they bump into me, elbow me like I was some object. And in Puerto Suárez that's the only thing that happens, they bump into you all the time. Bump into you and yell, offering to sell you crap. And all of it in that language of theirs, enough to drive you crazy.

A bunch of vendors in the streets, selling trinkets from China, batteries, junk of all kinds. Thanks to that, though, I managed to buy a tape player with earphones to hear the tapes Nei had given me.

Everything here is for shit, said a Brazilian I met in a restaurant. We waited five hours in the courtyard of the Federal Police, he said, closed tighter than a drum, nobody gave a damn about us. Everybody came and went as they pleased, crossing the border at will; no one asked for papers, passport, nothing, except I didn't want to cross that way, like a jerk, I practically forced those fuckers to give me a visa. Do you have a visa?

Yes, I lied. What do I do to buy a ticket?

It's hell, he answered. There's never anybody at the ticket window. The secret is to get up real early and camp out at the window.

The guy was drunk. I waited till he was distracted by a group of gringos coming into the restaurant and changed tables.

I ate quickly and found a hotel near the train station, with bath, three bolivianos a night.

I took a bath, cleaned Tiger, and stretched out on the bed with the photos I'd gotten from Nei. Érica and Samantha at the entrance to the hotel in Cuiabá. Marlênio in a church. Seeing that pretty boy aroused in me a different kind of hatred. It was a pleasant hatred. I loved that hatred. I enjoyed closing my eyes and feeling the hatred spread slowly from my mouth to the rest of my body like a drug. It gave me a certain peace, that hatred. The three of them coming out of a barbecue place in Manaus. Marlênio, showing all his teeth. He was even on the chubby side, the bastard. And Samantha holding their hands. Mama and Poppa. A happy family. The three of them. I wondered what Érica did with my twenty thousand dollars. Given it to that son of a bitch to open another church?

I wanted to listen to the tapes too, but I was tired. Érica, the bitch. How could she do that to me? Me, who took Érica out of the gutter, who gave her everything. A foolish, fucked-over girl without anywhere to live. Without anything.

I closed my eyes and went to sleep thinking about that. You can't be good in this world. Ever.

I woke up with a hard-on, someone taking off my undershorts, and suddenly I was fucking an enormous body with immense tits. Who's this fat woman? I thought, and only when I was coming did I remember the woman who took care of the reception desk and who'd come on to me. I didn't understand anything of what she said, only *usted*.

The worst thing about fucking like that, without wanting to, is that when it's over you want the woman to disappear. And then she starts saying *usted*.

I got up, dressed, and said I needed to leave. The fat woman didn't want to charge me, poor thing. I felt sorry for her. *Usted*. I insisted on paying. I even gave her a tip.

It was four in the morning. I imagined the number of guests she must fuck. Fat bitch. She'd bankrupt the hotel yet.

The ticket window didn't open till 6 a.m. I bought an intermediate-class ticket. The train wouldn't leave until three in the afternoon.

At ten that night, I got on board. The trip would take eighteen hours. If I got there alive, goddammit, if I got there alive and found Marlênio and Érica. God only knows what I was going to do to those two.

14

Sandals, Bermudas, T-shirt with a picture of Che Guevara, everything normal, discreet, cool, nothing special to make people laugh at me. I'm a fugitive. I don't like being stared at. I hate nosy types like the old man sitting next to me on the train. I'm always on the alert. He could be a cop, a detective, a con man. I'd been told that it's like that in Bolivia, guys always trying to put the squeeze on you.

Are you the type who picks up animals in the street? the old man asked. He'd been looking at me for some time. Two huge eyes on me and Tiger. Fingers stained yellow from cigarettes. It was the second question he'd asked me. The first was why I was taking a dog with me on the trip. Don't you think, he asked, that this train, this place, all of this, isn't appropriate for dogs?

Beats me. Hey, I wasn't the only one. There were passengers carrying chickens, ducks, pigs, even a monkey, despite it being forbidden to bring animals aboard. I don't know why the old man decided to single me out for a lecture.

He went on talking, saying that he was against picking up animals in the street. Dogs, he said, are no good for almost anything. They wander around, shitting and transmitting disease. They cause accidents. Rabies. If you want protection, a fence is better, an electrified entranceway. A fence doesn't eat up half your pay. Dogs are expensive, he said.

I told him that Tiger was all I had, but the old man wasn't listening.

When he finished talking about dogs, he started talking about potatoes. I have no idea what he thought about me. He explained that Bolivia had ten varieties of potato. And that it was potatoes that made Bolivian women look the way they did, like a sack of potatoes. Have you seen how fat they are?

At night it got a lot colder. The old man finally shut up. At the first stop, I saw there was no limit to the number of passengers; more people accommodated themselves on the floor.

I got the tape player and earphones and one of the tapes Nei had given me.

Tape 1

WOMAN: Hello?

ÉRICA: Enir?

WOMAN: Hello? Who's calling?

ÉRICA: Enir? It's me.

WOMAN: Bishop? I was hoping you'd call.

ÉRICA: We arrived safely, thank God. Listen, Enir. Did he show up?

WOMAN: Yes. He came here, just imagine, saying he was a music teacher.

Silence.

WOMAN: Bishop?

ÉRICA: I'm here. Was Máiquel there? Is that what happened?

WOMAN: He was at your house too. He went through everything there.

Pause.

ÉRICA: Who spoke to him there at the church?

WOMAN: Our worker, Paulo.

ÉRICA: The main thing, Enir, is for no one to say anything. Not about me, not about the Pastor, nothing.

WOMAN: We didn't give out any information at all. Just think, Bishop. We said there wasn't any Dona Érica here. Who's going to give information to the Devil?

ÉRICA: Did he ask about Marlênio?

WOMAN: We didn't say anything. Anything.

ÉRICA: What time was he there?

WOMAN: He knew about Samantha's guitar class. He was well informed.

ÉRICA: Did he say that?

WOMAN: What?

ÉRICA: How do you know he knew about Samantha's schedule?

WOMAN: The worker told us. He had information. Then he stayed outside, waiting for the class to end. He wanted to see if Samantha was in the group.

ÉRICA: My phone was tapped. He must have heard lots of our conversations.

WOMAN: What a scourge.

ÉRICA: We're going to La Paz now.

WOMAN: Leaving Brazil might be the best thing. He was after the girl at school. He didn't find out anything there either.

ÉRICA: I know. The school told me.

WOMAN: Yeah. You said this would happen one day.

ÉRICA: We were expecting it. We expect anything from that man.

WOMAN: Did they tell you he parked in front of the entrance to the school?

ÉRICA: They told me everything. I'd given the principal photos of him.

WOMAN: The police are really slow, aren't they, Bishop?

ÉRICA: But God's justice never fails.

WOMAN: What about Samantha?

ÉRICA: She's calmer now.

WOMAN: Is she aware of what's going on?

ÉRICA: I told her. Marlênio has spoken often with her. She's all right now, she understands it was best for us to go away.

WOMAN: That's important. She has to know the danger she's in.

ÉRICA:.   She's no longer a baby.

WOMAN: We had a wonderful service yesterday, with Pastor Ricardo.

ÉRICA: That's good. I'll call later, so we can talk more calmly.

WOMAN: Go with God, Bishop.

ÉRICA: Amen.

I saw that a man was looking at my luggage. To be on the safe side, I put my backpack in my lap.

Tape 2

ENIR: Hello?

MARLÊNIO: Enir?

ENIR: Hello?

MARLÊNIO: Enir, it's me, Pastor Marlênio. What's with this telephone? You never hear us!

ENIR: Pastor? I have a surprise for you. Do you know who arrived in town to visit us? Pastor Everaldo.

MARLÊNIO: How nice. Let me say a few words to him.

Pause.

ENIR: Is everything all right with all of you?

MARLÊNIO: Let me speak to the Pastor, Enir. I'm in a hurry.

MAN: Hello, brother. Your church is beautiful. I'm being treated very well.

MARLÊNIO: We're in Corumbá. We're going to Bolivia.

MAN: I know. Our people there are expecting your visit. Pastor Claudio is waiting for you.

MARLÊNIO: Érica is very upset, Pastor. Pray for us.

MAN: The poor sister! Tell her that possibilities for

missionary work in the region are vast. Pastor Claudio will orient you.

MARLÊNIO: We're not sure about anything. Érica is very nervous.

MAN: I know, I know. Enir explained the situation to me. That man –

MARLÊNIO: Is a criminal, a killer, wanted by the police.

MAN: I know, I know. But what I want to know is whether, as the child's biological father, he has any rights regarding her …

MARLÊNIO: He just wants our money. He wants to extort us.

MAN: Wouldn't it be a good idea for the Bishop to try to reach an agreement with him?

MARLÊNIO: There's no agreement possible. He's a criminal. A murderer.

MAN: Have you contacted the police?

MARLÊNIO: Of course. But we still don't feel safe. That man, Pastor Everaldo, is a professional killer. He's already killed I don't know how many.

I turned off the tape player. I stared out the window at the darkness outside.

I don't know why Anderson wanted me to hear that crap. Call me, he said, when you get to Santa Cruz. I'll have more information on Érica and Marlênio. Crap. I had a bad feeling, I barely managed to stay in my seat. That stuff was no good for me. No good at all.

★   ★   ★

Cold *chicha*, cold *chicha*. I woke up to the shouts of a woman who was moving among the passengers on the floor, carrying a bucket of some greenish liquid.

Don't drink it, said the old man, it's shit.

I was thirsty, so I drank some, and it wasn't bad.

They sold everything on that train. At each stop the Indians were stepped on by vendors who rushed in, offering fried chicken, roast, barbecue, candy, coffee, juice, that *chicha* stuff, and all kinds of crap.

I bought chicken. Tiger ate almost all of it.

The bathroom was in the last car, but I didn't even bother going there, I did what everybody did, I got out in the brush, with Tiger in my lap, and then we ran to overtake the train again. It was good to get some exercise.

I spent the rest of the afternoon listening to the tapes and looking at the photos Anderson had sent. There was one I couldn't stop looking at. Érica in slippers, a sleeveless dress, very slim, her hair pulled back, crossing the street, her head down, behind Marlênio and Samantha, who were walking hand in hand. In the photo, she was my Érica. The Érica I knew. I remembered the day we went into a bar where they played slow music.

Let's dance, she said.

We spun and spun and spun.

That girl, Cledir, is she your girlfriend? she asked.

She's a friend, I said.

I stuck my nose in Érica's neck and we continued like that, spinning, the people sleeping, waking up, going to work, and the two of us spinning. And later we walked home. Érica was playing, trying to keep her balance on the curb. When she looked like she was about to fall, I wrapped her in my arms, that was good.

And afterward, at home, she pulled me by my hair. Fuck me, she said, fuck me, and she grabbed my cock, and when she did that I felt a kind of stab in the heart, a good kind of stab.

But there were other tapes. The conversations. On one of the recordings she said, God forgive me, but what I want more than anything in the world is for that man to die. Shit, that really hurt. That Érica left, that she took Samantha and my twenty thousand dollars, I could understand all that. But to want me dead?

I bought coca leaves from a stoned Bolivian.

That one there fell off the train, the old man said. That's why he's all banged up.

I don't know if that was true. The guy really was fucked up.

Time passed very slowly on the train.

I chewed the leaves, gave some to Tiger. I'm going to try an experiment with you, Tiger, c'mere. Let's agree on something: if you understand what I'm saying, lay your head in my lap.

Tiger wagged his tail.

If I'm right, lay your head in my lap, I repeated. You took drugs and turned into a dog. Right?

Nothing.

Was it LSD?

Tiger laid his head in my lap.

144

I knew it. You shameless hippie. Well, I'm gonna tell you something, you mutt, and when I said that, I realized the old man was laughing. I didn't like it. An unpleasant guy. I couldn't even talk to my dog.

I spent the rest of the trip stretched out on the seat.

It was still eight hours to Santa Cruz.

15

The Train of Death isn't very big, and the station at Santa Cruz de la Sierra isn't very small, but they weren't made for each other, so the chances of you getting off in the woods is very high. That's what happened to me.

I didn't want to waste time. My plan was to go to the terminal and catch the first bus to La Paz.

I saw some playboys who were going to Cochabamba, drunk as skunks, and asked if I could split a taxi with them to the terminal. They were game. They couldn't stop laughing, their daddy paying for everything, it must be fun as hell. Six of us, plus Tiger, in a Monza stolen in Brazil. In fact, all the taxis there were Brazilian.

At the terminal, you're fought over by the transportation companies. A bunch of losers, the Bolivians. They shout at the top of their lungs when it's time to sell a ticket.

Don't buy it until you're sure the bus has a bathroom, said the old man on the train. All he thought about was pissing, that old man. It's going to be the worst trip of your life, believe me, he promised. And don't believe anything they tell you. All they do is lie. And plant coca. Bolivians are shit.

Luckily, I decided to call Anderson before going any further.

I'm in Santa Cruz, I said. I'm catching a bus to La Paz tonight.

There's been a change of plan, he said.

Shit, I was so tired. My legs ached, my arms too. Everything ached. Tiger looked at me, his tongue out. I don't know why, but I always felt sorry for Tiger. Fucked-up dog. More crippled by the day.

Érica's in Belém, he said after a pause.

I knew nothing was Anderson's fault, but I felt an enormous urge to smash his face. I looked at the sky, everything gray. It was cold.

What crap, I said, I came here for nothing.

Anderson said that Marlênio and Érica were alerted that the phone in the church in Campo Grande was tapped. What they don't know, continued Anderson, is that now we're tapping other phones too.

What hotel are they at?

The National. They're going to meet with the Curia.

What?

They're going to meet with the local scum. The bishops. There's going to be an important gathering in Belém. Evangelicals from all over Brazil.

I should've asked for details, tried to find out what had happened, but I simply stopped talking, lost the will.

I spend hours monitoring the conversation of those guys, said Anderson, and I never hear important things like the Last Judgment, glory on high, whatever, that shit. The fuckers never talk about God. They just talk about market share. And tithes. All they want from the census is to find out which state has the highest percentage of evangelicals. It's like that with Érica and Marlênio too, he said. They might actually be running away from you. They're scared shitless of you. But that's secondary. First, they're looking for a place to go on making money out the ass.

I didn't let Anderson finish talking. I hung up, discouraged. Shit, Belém. A fucking long way off. And I was too tired to go to Belém.

The proprietor of the hole where I was staying liked me. I think it was because I paid three days in advance. With great difficulty I got her to understand that I wanted to use the boarding house's video player. I gave her some money so I could take the equipment to my room.

After dinner, she and her daughter lugged the thing to my room. From its size, it must be old as hell. She said it was hers, the machine. I had already understood, but she kept repeating it. It was hers. It didn't belong to the guests. To get rid of them, I added some more change. *Gracias*. By now I was able to speak a few words in their language. *Buenos días. Hola! Qué tal?*

My hope was to discover a clue, something in that material.

After a bath, under the blanket, with Tiger on my lap, I watched Érica preach. One thing I had to admit, Érica had the knack. Who has something to offer to Jesus? she shouted in the midst of the faithful, all of them with both hands raised in the air. First they had sung a song, a kind of romantic music, corny, except that the loved one in this case was Jesus. Then another one, in which they jumped up and down, clapping their hands and stamping their feet, then finally Érica came on to fleece them. A thousand *reais*. The Holy Spirit, Érica said, told me to speak to you. I'm here to bring a message from the Holy Spirit. You watched the tape and believed she really did talk to the Holy Spirit. Know what the Holy Spirit told her? That it was necessary to convince the faithful to do their part, to donate to God ten per cent of what they earned. Who's going to offer five hundred *reais* to Jesus? That's the duty of each of us, she said. Because it's in the Bible. The faithful placed their donations in envelopes that the helpers distributed, while Érica gave her show. Impressive, Érica. A con artist, just like Marlênio. After all, she'd learned the drill. I want to know who's going to open their heart to Jesus Christ. One hundred *reais*. For the Devil, for fornication, for sins of the flesh, I see that many people give even a thousand *reais* a month. Fifty *reais*. But when I open the envelopes I see that people want to economize with Jesus. They say, Jesus, things are tight this month, forgive me, you know? I've already spent a lot on the Devil. I bought an expensive dress, Jesus. I spent it on my lover. On parties. I bought a pile of trinkets. I dropped the ball. This month, nothing for the Lord. Just a few pennies for the Lord. Everything went for booze, Jesus. For the Lord, who watches over me, my family, my health, I give only a pittance, for I spent the money on the Devil, who seeks my downfall. How can the Lord help you if you don't trust in Him? As the psalm says, trust in Him and He shall bring it to pass.

Many people, Érica continued, think that tithing is throwing money away. They think that it could be used to buy a blender. Some new clothes. Steak. Sausage. A cellphone. A pair of sneakers. A watch. Often, the guy doesn't tithe because there's a bill to pay. If I don't pay, he says, they'll cut off my electricity. I'll be in the dark, the poor man thinks. Now I say, because it was the Holy Spirit that told me to say it to you, that if you tithe, if you're a believer, there will be money to pay that bill. You won't lack for light. Your telephone won't be cut off. Nor will food be missing from your table. Jesus will provide. Jesus doesn't want your money. Jesus doesn't have any bills to pay. He doesn't need to buy a blender. Jesus doesn't need a new blouse. Jesus doesn't pay rent. Jesus wants only your faithfulness.

Érica and Marlênio pitilessly took those paupers' money. In another video the faithful offered 'whatever they had at the moment.' Give what you have now. Anything. Money, a gold chain, a ring, whatever you choose to offer. Show you're not attached to it, Érica said. I'd never seen such gall. I even saw people giving their eyeglasses.

After I turned off the video, I wondered whether Érica actually believed that crap. Or did she and Marlênio, when they counted the cash, laugh themselves silly?

When Lucia came into the room, I thought I was in the wrong place. Everything was wrong, I thought. The woman, the house. Especially me. A pair of legs to take your breath away. Everything about Lucia made you think of fucking, nothing else. That's what she said, without saying it. Black hair falling onto her shoulders, pretty. Pointed breasts in a T-shirt. White teeth. Skirt a little above the knee. Crossed legs.

Want some juice? she asked.

I don't deserve juice, I thought. Not from that woman.

I didn't understand anything the boy, her son, said, and vice versa.

He doesn't speak Portuguese, Lucia explained. I've been here for three years and I don't speak Portuguese with him.

Bronzed from the sun, but not like those pale-white women tourists who stretch out at the beach like lizards, she was naturally dark-skinned. Her toes, in her flip-flops, made me want to lick them.

So, how is Nei? she asked.

Good, I said, slaughtering cattle like mad.

She laughed. That bastard.

You know, she said, I feel sorry for him not being able to see his son. He misses his father, the boy. But that's life, isn't it?

She was mouth-watering, Lucia.

It was by accident that I decided to go to Lucia's house. In fact, I didn't even know her name was Lucia. But there's nothing to do in Santa Cruz. Everything closes at lunchtime.

I was walking in Plaza Veinte y Cuatro de Septiembre, looking for the iguanas in the trees, when I came across the boy's address in my pants pocket.

Because I didn't have anything to do, I decided to buy a wooden truck that they were selling in the square and pay the boy a visit.

I walked quite a bit to arrive at the place. I left the downtown area and entered a neighborhood full of wide streets, squares, and large old houses.

A skinny woman in a maid's uniform answered the door. I thought she must be Nei's ex-wife. But when I explained the situation, she led me to the living room, and that gorgeous woman appeared, Lucia.

What brings you to Santa Cruz? she asked.

I said I was just passing through. Business.

The boy stayed there, playing, for some time. Later he asked his mother for something. He wasn't interested anymore in the truck I'd brought him. He must have toys a lot better. Lucia called the maid, and the boy left, holding hands with the girl.

Would you like to drink something stronger? she asked when we were alone.

Lemonade is fine, I answered.

Lucia was standing, serving me. How did you meet Nei? she asked.

Well, Nei is the cousin of a friend of mine. I was already beginning to guess what Lucia's breasts and belly were like.

Beautiful hands, painted nails, a ring with a red stone.

Maybe I'll spend a few days in Santa Cruz, I said.

I said that because I knew, I was feeling, something was going to happen, that Lucia was interested, me too, that's how things begin.

I should've been ashamed of taking Lucia to a smelly boarding house like the one where I was staying, even more so after getting into her luxury car, but she found everything amusing, laughing at my stories, laughed when I told her, I'm a fugitive, I'm a killer and I'm traveling hundreds of miles after a son of a bitch that I want to kill.

Now tell the truth, she said.

It's true, I replied.

You don't have the face of a killer.

What kind of face do I have?

Drug dealer. Airplane pilot. That sort of thing.

Shit. Lucia thought I was part of her group.

We'd been partying for three days. She liked to snort, Lucia. And drink. She would bring blow to the boarding house, and whiskey, and we'd have a good time.

I still remember the first time she came up to the room. Fucking with all our clothes on. I grabbed Lucia at the door. I lifted her skirt, stuck my dick under the edge of her panties, holding her by the ass. She whispered in my ear, I'm going to come, and that made my legs shaky. I put Lucia on the bed and we spent the rest of the day fucking.

Lucia was scandalous, she'd laugh out loud, guffaw, talking dirty, but when she came, she would whisper.

Another good thing about Lucia was that she liked cock. She saw right away that I had a star tattooed there. Not all women noticed. There are women who like to fuck, who like a dick between their legs, but don't like cock. I mean, don't like to touch it. Or suck it. That wasn't the case with Lucia.

Why'd you get that tattoo?

I told her it had been because of Érica.

I'm older than you, she said, I'm going to tell you a little secret: when you're in bed with a woman, a pretty woman like me, don't talk about other women. It's not nice, understand? Make up some shit. Lie. Say it was a vow to Our Lady of Aparecida.

You asked, I said.

That doesn't mean I want to know the truth. I'm not a scientist. Or your wife. We're here to have a good time, understand?

I understand. It was a vow.

She was cool, Lucia. She really knew what was what.

At the end of the afternoon, Lucia would go home to her son, pick up some clothes, and around ten at night return with all sorts of things. Look what I brought: whiskey, some stuff to snort, and munchies so we won't have to go out. It's not a good idea to flaunt it, Santa Cruz is a small town. Everybody knows everybody else, you know?

Where's your boyfriend? I asked. Doesn't he mind your spending the night away from home?

Juan is away, she said.

What if he shows up?

Well, he'll beat the crap out of you.

Jesus, I was in no mood to get the crap beat out of me.

Isn't it better, then, for you to go home?

Lucia was jerking her boyfriend's chain, and this was the story. After two years of marriage to Nei, with a still young child, she met a pilot in Corumbá, a drug trafficker, and fell in love. It wasn't Juan yet. It was somebody else. But she ran off to Santa Cruz with the pilot. They stayed together for a year, until she met Juan, who was one of the drug kingpins of the area.

I'm not his only lover. He has others, the bastard. Right now, for example, he must be in La Paz, snorting with some Indian woman.

Time to get out of Santa Cruz, I saw. I said I was leaving for Belém, to settle accounts with a guy.

I think I can help you, she said. Maybe a friend of mine can give you a lift.

But fuck me first, she said.

Lucia smelled good. It wasn't perfume, it was her.

No, she said when I grasped her around the back. I want to come in your mouth.

Meet me at the Dumbo ice-cream parlor, next to the church, at three. Today you're going to see an iguana. Kisses, Lucia. The note was on the pillow.

I hadn't seen Lucia get up, she didn't make any noise, I guessed she'd gone home during the night, to be able to take her son to school.

It was ten in the morning, and I didn't have the foggiest idea of what to do until three. I got Tiger from the bathroom and fed him chocolate.

Santa Cruz has seven hundred and thirty thousand inhabitants. That's what was written in the brochure they leave on the nightstand for tourists. *The second largest city in Bolivia.* Big fucking deal. *One thousand five hundred and fifty feet in altitude.*

Climate: pleasant and unusual. Goddamn unusual, that's for sure. I could even understand their language. But only to read; when they spoke, shit, what a language.

I showered, put on clean clothes, and left with Tiger for the city.

16

Lucia picked up the cherry on top of the ice cream and stuck it in my mouth. She said that was her favorite thing to do, have a strawberry-and-chocolate sundae at the Dumbo. Order one for yourself, she said. It's only eight hundred calories and they all go straight to your ass.

I had just taken a walk through the city with Tiger, actually not a walk, I explained to Lucia as soon as I got to the square. Tiger was a real handful, stopping all the time, limping, dragging his butt, he must be in pain. Hat, sunglasses, Lucia looked like an actress.

He's really in bad shape, Lucia commented. And I've got dark circles under my eyes because of you, she said, taking off the glasses and showing me her eyes. Fucking causes circles under the eyes.

There weren't any dark rings under her eyes.

They haven't invented a cosmetic that does away with

it. The best thing is cucumber. I spent all morning with cucumber slices on my eyes and it didn't do any good.

You're beautiful, I said.

I took her hand. We remained silent, sharing the sundae and looking at the Dumbo painted on the wall, which had nothing to do with Walt Disney's chubby and idiotic elephant. It was all twisted. Looked like Tiger.

After we finished the ice cream, Lucia told me that everything was taken care of. You're leaving tomorrow morning.

It made me feel good to have Lucia handling my life. Suddenly, she was calling the shots. And soon she'd disappear. Like all the other women. Like Érica, Cledir, Eunice. I'd never see Lucia again. Deep down, it doesn't matter what you do, no one is left. Everything ends. They end it for you. They put things in the way. Life itself. Or nothing. It just doesn't work. You yourself try to destroy it. Because the hard thing isn't loving. It's seeing it through. Moving ahead. Living together, every day. Sometimes you only realize what was good after you've already destroyed everything. When it comes to love, it doesn't end that way, like some corpse, it ends much worse. In a coat and tie. In the church. With children. Full of dregs. That's where things start to really stink. But with Lucia I didn't run that risk. Lucia also had a very clear idea about love, and it had to do with the price of the creams she used. And with the role of men at home. Someone to change light bulbs. And hammer nails, like she'd said in bed. You don't need a husband to do that. It can be a plumber, an electrician. And the same person who pays for my creams can pay my plumber. It's the advantage, she'd said, of not being twenty years older. No more illusions, you know? You see, you don't need a man around the house. My business now, Lucia had said, has more to do with bills to be paid than anything else. So, with Lucia it was only this itself. Those moments. That ice cream. Only that, and I should make the most of it.

I'm talking about a super serious matter, and you're not even listening.

Of course I'm listening.

Then repeat it.

I'm leaving tomorrow.

Right. A friend of mine, Ronnie, continued Lucia, is going to give you a ride.

Your boyfriend.

My ex.

If I were your boyfriend, you wouldn't have a string of lovers, I said.

That's what all of you say.

I would fuck only you.

Only me. I know. I believe it. The ideal man.

She took a pack of mints from her purse and stuck one in my mouth. She was trying to stop smoking. She explained that Ronnie was a good guy. You just have to settle a few details with him. I agreed we'd meet him at the church in a little while. As a matter of fact, she said, looking at her watch, it's time right now.

★   ★   ★

When we went into the church, Ronnie was there waiting for us, sitting in the last pew. Around his neck, a thick gold chain. These guys with a little dough, but not that much, are all alike. The first thing they buy, from what I've seen, is that chain. It must be in the manual on how to get ahead in life. First stage, buy a gold chain. That comes before the car. That way, those with less dough know you've moved up a step. That you're not some loser like them. You're at step one. His chain was very thick. Step one, with honors.

How's it going, man? he asked, simpatico, when Lucia introduced us.

We didn't even have time to start a conversation. A priest or somebody like one came furiously toward us, complaining.

Lucia explained to me that it was because of Tiger. Dogs can't enter a church, she said. Can't you leave the animal outside?

I didn't like her impatient tone. I would rather have left with my dog. But I did what she asked.

So you want a ride? Ronnie asked when I returned.

Lucia said you could help me, I said. I kept watching the door, afraid that Tiger would come in again and annoy the crow, who was now cleaning the altar and looking sidelong at us. I don't like priests.

It's one favor for another. I'm heading to Porto Velho. Then I'll take you to Belém.

I asked what my part was.

Providing my security for a delivery.

A simple thing, Lucia added. Nothing that you don't know how to do.

If that's it, I said, I'm in.

We talked a bit more, trivial stuff.

I was about to get up when Ronnie added a condition. I couldn't take the dog.

Why? I asked.

He gets in the way, he said. It won't work.

Shit. I got even madder at the crow. I had already noticed something. In the world, what matters is the rule of the flock. The pack. Nobody thinks. But if one of them barks, the others start barking too. They attack together. Without knowing what's going on. It was because of the crow that Ronnie was acting that way. He didn't know it, but he was.

Lucia, Ronnie asked, can you send the dog to one of Juan's ranches?

She agreed.

Then it's settled. It'll be better for him.

Lucia knew the whole story of my dog. I have no idea what she'd told Ronnie, but the fact is the pilot hadn't understood shit. Or Lucia either. I wasn't about to leave Tiger in the hands of Bolivians. No fucking way. Without me, he wouldn't last a week. Who was going to take care of an ugly piece of meat like him? Old. Lame. Wherever he went, he'd be in for it. On Juan's ranch, who knows but what right off they'd put a bullet in him? I won't do that to a dog. Or a child. Or a pregnant woman. It's a rule. There are some things a man ought not to do. Dumping him like that. Without mercy.

I thanked him and said that without the dog I wasn't going.

I was already getting up when Ronnie came after me.

Okay, he said. We leave early tomorrow. But one more thing. You know how to handle guns, don't you?

Shit. What a laugh.

He left the church first. Lucia and I stayed behind inside for a short time longer. Ronnie doesn't like to hire outside help, she explained. It was only then that I understood I was being hired.

In the square, Lucia gave me a peck on the cheek and said ciao. Just like that, like I was nobody. Take care, she said.

Hold on a minute, I said, grabbing her arm. I thought we were going back to the boarding house. I wasn't leaving till late at night, I explained.

Juan's arrived, she said. I can't stay with you.

But are we going to say goodbye like this? Just a ciao and that's it?

She laughed.

I'm sorry. The boss is at home.

I saw Lucia walk to her car. Swinging her hips. Smiling. She simply left. Happy as could be. I stood there, not knowing what to do. Horny as hell. Shit. Women are goddamm rotten. They have no heart.

We know you're a fugitive. We know you killed your wife. We know you killed a shitload of people. We know you killed a cop in São Paulo. That you were the partner of a corrupt police detective. Dude, we even know what color shorts you're wearing, said Ronnie, when I asked how he knew I had a security firm. Actually, he said, Lucia dug up almost everything by herself. She called Nei, who called I don't know who. All I did was the fine tuning. You think Lucia was going to put a guy in my plane she barely knows? Lucia is the Man's woman. And, dude, don't be naive, continued Ronnie, the Medellín cartel even has American policemen working for them. You think we're far behind?

We were flying in his Cessna. In place of the rear seat, which had been yanked out, two drums, one of ether and one of acetone. Tiger made himself comfortable on top of them.

I had never traveled to those parts. Ronnie flew low. I have to avoid the Americans, he said. There's DEA radar around here.

Up there, you could see the holes in the forest.

Know where that wood goes? Ronnie asked. China, Japan, Taiwan, and South Korea. The best of whatever we have goes there.

In some stretches, you believed you were really flying over the rainforest. But that was just an impression. When Ronnie descended a bit further, a lot of clearings appeared, where the trees had been ripped out. The best, said Ronnie. The most important. It's normal. They cut down everything.

Besides that, we saw several burns and soy fields.

After two hours of flying, we descended onto a clandestine airstrip. Two Bolivians greeted us, and all they asked me to do was help carry the drums to a shed used to refine the coca. Was this the favor I was supposed to do? I felt encouraged.

If that's all there was to it, it was an ideal job.

Ronnie liked talking about his life, and I kept egging him on.

If there's anything in life that bugs me, he said, it's getting caught in some lousy trap. Like marriage, property tax, life insurance, that kind of thing. You pay and pay and pay. And you still owe. And then you make another payment. And the next month you pay again. I'd rather not pay and not have anything. I live in hotels, and when I get tired of a place, I move. I've got money in my pocket. If I get sick, I go there and pay the doctor. I don't use checks. Or credit cards. None of that's any good. To me, the thing has to be in cash. Here and now. Once you start paying installments, you're already dead and don't know it. I don't pay. I've never built a house. I don't like anything that's definite. I'm gonna die, and the house stays behind? What for? Our business has its advantages, he said, when we were in the air again.

The bad part was Ronnie's laugh that came with the stories. And the cough and the spitting, I had to turn away. A filthy guy, Ronnie.

It's really a good business, he said, when I asked about the market. None better. In Brazil, we snort a lot these days. That stuff about only the poor doing drugs is bullshit. Maybe in Europe cocaine is out of fashion with the upper crust. You hear that nowadays the beautiful people don't like to shoot up anymore or get smashed, they prefer to save endangered species, the whales, or solve the problem of the planet's water supply. But here our rich people are still on the fuck-you system. They're still assholes, that's for damn sure. They're corrupt, thieves, coke snorters. And the drug trade lives off that, off bad people. Off pieces of crap, like our politicians. Off shits who think of nothing but how to

164

steal. And our poor are assholes too. They also steal. And kill. Except that, unlike the rich, they go to jail. But it takes a long time, because our justice system is slow. That's why the drug trade here has become such big business. Basically, our people are no damn good. And they snort like mad. Everybody snorts.

I asked Ronnie if he'd introduce me to the kingpins.

To the kingpins? You?

Ronnie thought about it.

It depends, he said after a time. Maybe we can come to an arrangement. First you have to show me what you can do.

I didn't answer.

In Porto Velho it was hard to land because of the smoke from the burns, which didn't let you see hardly anything.

I'm used to it, Ronnie said. It's always like this.

When the visibility improved, he landed.

One thing there's no shortage of in Porto Velho is holes. There's few trees. Few squares. Dirty bars. An ugly city.

At the airport, Ronnie rented a car, and from there we went to Mocambo, where his brother lived. Apparently Adailson wasn't too happy about us arriving unexpectedly. Or about Ronnie showing up with me and Tiger. He was wary.

I'm going to take you to a good restaurant, Ronnie said, walking into the house without ceremony. Go put on some decent clothes.

Don't we look a lot alike? Ronnie asked later, during the lunch at a restaurant beside the river. And they did. Big ears, both of them. Dark complexion. With blue spots around the eyes. That really was a case of circles under the eyes.

Ronnie was the type who got all mushy when he drank. He told his brother, You know that I fucking love you, man. I love this kid, he said to me.

I find such family scenes unpleasant.

I buried my head in the menu. *Maniçoba, a typical dish of the region made with cooked maniva leaves, a plant known as cassava in the south of the country. Caruru.* Could that be the slimy yellow stuff the man at the next table was eating?

Have a *tucunaré* stew, Adailson said when the waiter came to take our order.

I didn't know what that was, but I went along.

For dessert, we ate compote of *cupuaçu.*

Now and then, Ronnie would lower his voice and speak to his brother. How much did you make on that? Open up to me, he said. I'm on your side. I can only help you if you tell me what happened.

Real strange, those two. Tiger sensed the sinister atmosphere, so did Adailson, the guy was dying to get out of there but couldn't. Brazil was playing Chile that afternoon.

Let's watch the game together, Ronnie said.

We stopped at a supermarket, bought beer, and returned to Mocambo.

Adailson's TV was one of those you only see in ads, flat screen, stereo, vivid colors, it drove Ronnie wild. Where'd you get the money for that gizmo, Adailson?

I locked myself in the bathroom with Tiger and went through the medicine cabinet; I didn't want to witness the scene between the two of them. Medicine for headaches. For the stomach. For athlete's foot. For hemorrhoids. The two of them were boiling over. Slaps. You gonna tell me or not? shouted Ronnie. Medicine for fungus. Anti-dandruff shampoo. I didn't like for people to rummage around in my bathroom medicine cabinet. I always kept junk there, so nobody could spy on me. It's a real drag for someone to find out you've got mange. Adailson was really falling apart. Medication for everything.

Máiquel, Ronnie shouted, it's starting.

When I entered the living room, they had settled the argument. Silent at first.

Grab a beer, Máiquel. Sit over there. Relax.

They lit a joint, and suddenly they were both feeling good, hugging, yelling, rooting. More beer, more grass. Five goals. One hell of a game.

Ronnie started the car, drove to the corner, and stopped. He looked at his brother's house in the rear-view mirror. Then he took a gun out of the glove box and handed it to me.

Go back there, he said, and kill Adailson. He didn't even let me open my mouth. Go in and say you have to use the bathroom, he said. Or that you forgot your wallet. As soon as he turns his back, shoot. Just once, in the head. I don't want him to suffer.

Dude, I said, he's your brother.

Then Ronnie collapsed onto the steering wheel, sobbing like a child. Forgive me, God, he said. Forgive me.

I didn't get out of the car. I was hoping Ronnie would change his mind.

After a time, still crying, he asked me was I going to do the job or not.

I didn't want to kill anybody. That wasn't what we'd agreed on.

Are you going to make me put a bullet in my own brother?

I looked at him, not answering. A grown man that size, crying. Fuck.

Are you? he shouted. You piece of shit. Are you going to do that to me?

I got out of the car, fucking mad.

No idea what the guy had done. But that was why I'd been brought there. Now I understood. Abilities. Fuck. This was the price of the ride. Things like that cost dearly, I should know that.

17

We almost didn't speak during the trip to Belém. Ronnie wasn't feeling well, he was sweating a lot, he even vomited into a plastic bag.

He didn't ask me about his brother's death, and I was relieved not to have to say that everything went down different from my plan. My idea, as I headed for Adailson's house, in the sun, with my belly full of *tucunaré* and beer and my head spinning from marijuana, was to make up some lie and get the hell out of there.

I thought I could resolve everything by talking. Misdirecting. But as soon as I entered the house Adailson jumped onto my back. The guy was crazy. I just wanted to talk to him and get away. Explain that I wasn't going to do anything to him. They want to kill you, I was going to say. Your brother and the Bolivians. I just came to warn you. I don't know what you did, I was going to alert you, run away, get out of here. But he was like some crazy animal, caught me in a stranglehold, tried to choke me, kicked me, cursed, I wrenched myself free, and when I did I saw that Adailson had a knife in his hand. I shot him three times in the belly, fuck. That was it. Very fast.

When I returned, Ronnie must have noticed I had a cut on my forehead. I don't even know how I cut myself. It must've been when Adailson grabbed me from behind.

Now I felt sick myself and wanted to get out of that airplane as soon as possible. Get away.

To make things worse, Ronnie started talking nonsense about how much he loved his brother, how he'd always looked out for his brother, shit, a real sob story. If you didn't kill Adailson, he said, they would have. Them. The kingpins. They never forgive. There's no pardon in our job. You fuck up, you're dead. And me, Ronnie said, I'm nothing. I just carry things from there to here. I'm just the pilot. A beast of burden. They're the ones giving the orders. They were going to cut out Adailson's tongue. You know what they do to traitors? They bury them alive. But first they torture them. With a blowtorch. That's what they do to traitors. Nobody gets away with deceiving those guys, understand?

Okay, now I felt better.

At the airport in Belém, I got my backpack, got Tiger. Thanks for the lift, I said.

I got in a taxi and left. A cheap hotel, I told the driver. Real cheap.

★   ★   ★

I spent ten minutes under the shower to clear my head. Bang, bang, and the man crumbled. Not all at once like a rotten jackfruit, he fell like an imploding building, in slow motion, taking an enormous amount of time, and I saw it all, which was the worst part.

I had no reason to kill Adailson. My business was with Marlênio. That was the guy I had to kill. Marlênio was the one who had fucked everything up. Until he came along, my life was going great. He was the one who put ideas in Érica's head. He was the one who ratted me out. He was the one who was living large now, with money out the ass. And I had just put three slugs in Adailson's belly. If Ronnie had problems with Adailson, if Adailson was a traitor, fuck 'em. Why had I gotten involved in that story?

I was mad as shit at Ronnie. One more corpse. I turned off the shower.

Afterward, I stretched out on the bed, with the fan on, and stayed there, hugging my dog.

I had a lot of things to do, call Anderson, look for Érica, but I decided to keep quiet, cooling my head. I turned on the TV and ordered a cheese sandwich, a Coca-Cola, a chunk of ham for Tiger, and collapsed into bed.

I was tired as shit.

The elevator door opened. Marlênio sitting in the hotel lobby, with a lot of people around him. The problem is to hit the head, I thought. I didn't want to scatter the brains of the guy next to him.

I couldn't hear what Marlênio was saying, which was good; just seeing the tie, the shoes of the preacher, I could feel the poison spreading through my entire body. Don't lose control, I told myself. I closed my eyes and listened to my own breathing.

No need to hide, someone told me. How long have you been after that guy? It was only there, in the lobby, that I realized, fuck it, I thought, whatever happens from here on out doesn't matter. I just wanted to see who was speaking to me. But there wasn't anyone there. You can even get arrested. Your objective is to put a bullet between that guy's eyes. It'll be good if everyone knows. Especially Érica. Now I was the one talking aloud. To myself. Everybody in the lobby heard my voice. I was the one saying everything.

I took a few steps. It's really me, I said. People looked at me. Tell Érica, I said. Tell her I was here.

I saw a woman running. I heard gunshots. Two. That man's been hit, someone said.

But I hadn't fired yet. The gun, I saw, wasn't with me. Blood began spurting from my belly. Marlênio was in front of me. He went on talking to people, calm, like nothing had happened. The bastard looked at me and laughed. Shit. He doesn't die, that faggot.

I woke with the sun in my face. I closed the windows. I went back to the bed and called Anderson. I wanted to make sure that Érica and Marlênio were at the National Hotel.

I can't talk now, he said. Give me the number where you are and I'll call you in five minutes.

Want the news? he said when he called back. Go to the bank and pay me what you owe me. I don't work for free even for good-looking women. We'll talk after you make the deposit.

A mercenary guy, that Anderson. I called again, trying to explain the situation. I'm out of time, I said.

And I'm out of money, he replied, hanging up in my face.

Anderson was a real miser.

At eleven o'clock I was in the street. Ninety-one degrees. In Belém, the first thing you want to do when you leave the hotel is go back to the hotel. The mango trees scattered around the city don't do much to relieve the heat. You walk for three minutes and feel cooked on the inside, your flesh weak. Rotten things come out of your head. Your brain practically shuts down. Your insides too. Whatever you eat sits there, fermenting, for good. That's how I functioned in Belém.

Good thing I didn't take Tiger with me. I left him in the room, resting; the poor thing wouldn't be able to take walking in that heat.

At the reception desk at the National Hotel I introduced myself as a pastor of the Powerful Heart of Jesus, saying I had an appointment with Bishop Marlênio.

The receptionist fiddled with the computer and said the hotel had no one by that name registered.

There must be some mistake, I said. Check again. I put ten *reais* on the counter.

The man hammered on the computer again.

No one by that name, he said after a time.

I put ten more *reais* on the counter. And I gave Érica's name.

173

Another employee came to help, all smiles. It was the manager. He remembered Bishop Marlênio and his wife. They were with us for a week, he said. Very nice people. A lovely little daughter. They visited the island of Marajó before leaving. They checked out two days ago, he said. He didn't know anything more.

That's all I got, by paying. Politeness.

From there, I walked until I found a bank where I could make Anderson's deposit. Deducting the five hundred, I had fifteen hundred left. For the time being, I didn't have anything to worry about. I mean, except the accident still got to me, Adailson slowly crumbling before my eyes.

At the hotel, I found Tiger sleeping in front of the fan. While I took off my sweat-soaked shirt, I phoned Anderson.

I told him that Érica and Marlênio weren't at the National anymore and that the manager himself had told me they'd left the city two days ago.

You have to look for the evangelical church Jesus Gathers His Flock in the Flowered Garden of Liberation, Anderson said.

What a name, I said.

There are worse. That church is Bishop Otávio Freitas's. He's the one who invited Marlênio and Érica to go to Belém.

Anderson had already told me the story of that moneybags; he was repeating it needlessly. He's the one who began preaching in morgues, remember? Today he owns ten churches, radio and TV programs. It's not hard to locate the guy in Pará. Find Otávio and you'll find those two.

I was getting irritated with Anderson. Érica and Marlênio

always got away. It seemed like their Anderson was better than mine.

I forgot to mention one thing, he said. I heard a conversation between a church employee and a police detective from Mato Grosso. They're after you too. A plan is being put together. I don't know what it is, it was never explained, but stay on your toes. There's money behind this. They think you're still in Corumbá. They paid for the police to haul you in. Marlênio wants to see you dead, any way possible.

What are you going to do? Anderson asked.

I'm going to find Marlênio, I said. Any way possible.

Dredges. Unfinished works. Motel Darling. Shanty towns. Lamp posts. Building materials. Junk yard. Package store. And also enormous posters, along with other ads for credit cards and naked women that said: *Jesus is talent. Remove My Heart People Abode.* What did that mean? *Murmur, they tell me, Jesus, iniquity kills. Corruption Jesus.* A dark world in flames. Gruesome posters. I'd seen others like them in other cities. I mean, in the poor parts of the cities. Shanty towns and Jesus, on the outskirts. I have no idea what that meant. I didn't understand anything. Actually, I think that was the idea, to confuse. Or scare people. Anybody's guess.

From the window of the bus I looked for the place to get off. The fare collector had said three stops after the intersection of the avenues.

There it is, he said, seeing that I was lost.

I got off. The evangelical church Jesus Gathers His Flock in the Flowered Garden of Liberation was impressive. It looked like a Wal-Mart of God. In terms of size. An entire square block.

Anderson told me that morning that Otávio Freitas had dozens of them. Not as large. Actually, this was the largest. In the rest of the state of Pará, it's all a simple thing, Anderson said. The guy's as crafty as they come, he keeps his eye on everything; when they start clearing a plot of land, he goes ahead, and when the people arrive, he's already there, ready to pounce. Otávio Freitas is one of those who thinks a church is like indoor plumbing. To him, a city has to have a bank, sewers, running water, McDonald's and evangelical Quonset huts.

I arrived at the church just as the faithful were giving their testimony.

A lady told how her life had gotten better after she entered the Flowered Garden of Liberation. She was totally broke and owed two thousand *reais* to the Housing Bank. She couldn't ask for a bank loan because the Apostle says one must not borrow money and pay interest. Glory to God in the name of the Lord. My husband was in jail, the lawyer took everything we had. That was when I came to the church and Pastor Otávio told me, Believe in the God who will cleanse your name. My name was sullied. And what happened? That same day, God cleansed my name. The bank manager called me saying that money had appeared in my account. To this day no one can explain it. Two thousand *reais*.

Shit, I thought. All that's missing now is Santa Claus.

Are you new here? asked a woman in blue, very pretty, who worked at the church.

I'm a police investigator, I said.

Are you getting acquainted with our church?

I need to talk to Bishop Otávio Freitas. It's an urgent case.

Her expression changed immediately.

Can you please come with me.

We went to a room behind the stage.

Three muscular men joined us there, and we waited for the service to end. From there we could hear the singing, the weeping, the sermon.

Our misfortune as Brazilians, said the preacher, was not being colonized by the Hebrews. Or by the Germans. The Dutch. We'd be rich, he said. We'd be First World. The problem in Brazil is the Catholic Church. A country like ours, poor, with so much inequality, the Catholic Church arrives, and what does it do? It implants religious holidays. It's one holiday after another. God has no way to help the Brazilian. Because of all the holidays.

After that, more singing.

Ten minutes later, a mulatto pastor came to talk to me. His name was Edmundo. Right off he said that Bishop Otávio couldn't see me but that he personally would be very happy to help me.

I introduced myself as Rogério da Silva Pereira, police investigator. I told a long, involved story about how I was working with Detective Saulo, from Mato Grosso, on the case of a professional killer named Máiquel. A very complicated case. And very dangerous. And I greatly needed the cooperation of our friend the Pastor. I said we had lost the killer's trail in Corumbá but that now we'd been informed that he was in Belém. We're trying to get in touch with Mr Marlênio, a friend of Bishop Otávio Freitas. We fear his life may be in danger.

It's incredible how dumb people are. They right away get shit-scared. The preacher didn't even ask me for ID.

He quickly told me everything. He said that Bishop Marlênio and Bishop Érica were with Bishop Otávio on a pleasure cruise and would be in Manaus in a few days for an evangelical conference to discuss missionary work. The guy was like an open faucet.

I left there with all the information I wanted, including a brochure about the evangelical conference with the name of the hotel where they'd be staying. Edmundo also gave me his cellphone number and wrote down the false number that I gave him. Let's keep in touch, we agreed.

Finally, Edmundo asked whether he should alert Bishop Otávio, send a radio or phone message to the boat.

Don't frighten anyone, I said. But ask them to get in contact with me. Say that a detective from Mato Grosso wants to talk to them, only that. And urgently.

I thanked him and left.

As dumb as they come, that guy. Impressive.

18

Meat, perfume, refrigerators, junk for voodoo, craftwork, fish, clothes, pots, fruit, food, cooking utensils, plants to help you find a husband, everything is for sale at the Belém market. Even vulture liver. It's to quit drinking, explained the man at the stall. I myself stopped, I've never since put a drop of booze in my mouth, he said. But I noticed he still reeked of alcohol. Horrible breath.

I'd been wandering around there since noon. That morning I had gotten up early, checked out of the hotel and gone straight to the port, with Tiger limping behind me. The boat to Manaus wasn't leaving till six, there was no point in waiting. I bought the ticket and went for a walk around the city.

I passed by the Docks station, walked slowly to the Ver-o-Peso market, beside the Castelo fort. Horrible heat, everything humid, sticky. It hurt me to see Tiger under that sun. From time to time, I would stop to let him rest.

At the market, I found a bar, in the shade, and we stayed there, looking at the fishing boats, the canoes, the tourists, the confusion of the stalls. I'd never seen anything like it. The women actually screamed. One of them was putting curlers in another's hair. When a customer arrived, the one in curlers would get up and start selling fruit. Assai palm, *cupuaçu*, bacury, soursop, sapodilla, guava, mangoes, cashews, and cabbage trees. Bellowing. Disorderly.

The bar owner convinced me to try *tacacá*, a slimy goo of manioc, shrimp, and pepper. After serving me, he sat down beside me, and we stared at the woman in curlers. Ugly as sin.

One of the causes of separations, he said, has to be curlers. Curlers also end marriages. As much as drinking. As much as cheating. I shudder every time I look at that woman. Things like that ought to be forbidden. By law.

Places like the Ver-o-Peso market made me think of Eunice. She would've bought all sorts of things. The names of all the miracle-working plants were scrawled on small cards: *bring-you-to-me, cry-at-my-feet, take-me-and-never-let-me-go, clutched-tight*, and many others. A few young women gathered in front of the witches, wanting to know how to use the herbs. All you had to do was write the name of the loved one on a piece of paper, fold it, wad it up, put it in the vial with the herbs and run it over your body, but always from bottom to top, explained one of the women running the stall.

There was a remedy for anything, betrayal, separation, adultery, loneliness, plantar warts, mange, boils, the evil eye, everything. Dry the leaves in the sun, then crush them up until they become a fine powder, and put it in his food. I only heard pieces of the explanations. Rub it on every day. Cook it with everything in it. Cut and dice into small pieces. Then throw everything away. The man will turn into a lamb, the witches said. The scales will fall away. The foreign women didn't understand the first thing, but they bought.

Secrets of love. Hold your man for life, said a placard with colored letters. In front of it, a lot of small vials with a piece of something inside.

What's that? I asked.

The old woman explained it was pussy from a female river dolphin. Not in those words. It's the dolphin's thingy, she said. And any woman who used it would drive her man wild. You had to melt it in a double boiler and rub it on your cunt before fucking.

If your girlfriend uses it, she said, you're lost.

I bought some to send to Eunice. Just for the hell of it.

I've been here for thirty years, said the old black woman as she put my present in a plastic bag. I've seen cures for everything in this place. I've seen cripples walk, seen people with cancer be healed, seen the blind start to see, but there's one thing nobody can solve. How to get rid of the thieves that infest the market. The swindlers. The lowlifes. Careful with your money. It's full of guys robbing my customers.

It was true. I'd already seen gringos being held up. I myself had stolen. Actually, I didn't rob. A German made it too easy, he dropped his wallet at the place where I had the *tacacá*. I picked it up, a hundred and fifty bucks. Lucky. I increased my capital.

I also bought a small wheeled cart from a kid hanging out in the market. On the Train of Death a veterinary student had suggested I adapt one of those carts to Tiger's hind legs. It'll work like a wheelchair, the guy said. Maybe he'll feel better.

On the way to the port, carrying the cart and the dolphin pussy, I called the supermarket where Eunice worked.

Did something happen? she asked.

No. I'm in Belém.

Did you find the kidnapper?

I'm going to Manaus. I think she's there. With my daughter.

Shit, that slut is leading you a merry chase, isn't she?

I bought you a present, I said.

My boss is here, I don't have time for small talk. Say what you've got to say.

Don't you want to know what it is?

What?

The present I bought for you.

No.

It's river-dolphin pussy.

What are you talking about?

The cunt of the female dolphin. The fish.

That's disgusting. You're disgusting.

The women here in Belém use it. To drive their boyfriends wild.

You're depraved. Is that what you called to tell me?

They apply it before fucking.

Máiquel, you know very well that I married a cool guy.

182

Know what I think, Eunice? That your husband doesn't exist.

What?

Just what I said. You didn't get married.

Of course I got married. In a wedding gown and veil. A religious ceremony and a civil one. My husband's the greatest guy. My girlfriends here are dying of envy. This weekend we went to Petrópolis, it was super cool. He loves me, Máiquel.

When I finish what I have to do, I'll come visit you. I want to see if it's true.

If I were you, I wouldn't show up here. My husband is very jealous. He'll beat you up if you come to Nova Iguaçu. Friendly advice.

I miss you.

That's your problem. I'm happy as a clam.

Silence.

Eunice, don't you?

Don't I what?

Miss us. Miss me.

You?

Yeah. I miss you. The two of us. Sometimes I close my eyes and remember us fucking.

Fucking is all you think about. That's your problem. There are other things than fucking. There's real life, you know, Máiquel? Working hard. Earning a living. Spending all day here at the supermarket checkout counter, ringing up steel wool and chicken. That's real life.

Fucking you is great.

There are better things in life than fucking.

Like what?

Friendship. Commitment.

I started laughing.

You didn't get married, I said. I know you didn't get married.

Oh crap. Why don't you stop calling me?

You'd like it here, I said.

I like an honest man, Máiquel. That's what I like. You're not my type. Go after Érica. She's just like you. My manager's coming, ciao.

She hung up in my face. But first she said ciao. In her own way, but she said it.

I stuck the vial with the dolphin pussy in my pocket. If I could, I planned to send it by mail. Though I didn't have her address anymore. Could Eunice really have gotten married? To a loser? To a guy who carried her bag while she went shopping at the street fair? I always used to see jerks doing that. The wife in front, looking annoyed, buying beans, and the husband behind, carrying her bag. Shit. What a drag, Eunice married.

I returned to the port area at a quarter of five. I didn't want to miss the boat to Manaus. No fucking way.

The only long stop, I found out, would be in Santarém, the rest, Almeirim, Prainha, Monte Alegre, Óbidos, and Juruti, were just for loading and unloading of passengers. In five days I'd be in Manaus. Very good. That was exactly what I wanted. A bit of peace. To see the Pará River and the Amazon. From the hammock. See alligators and piranhas. Eat fish. Sleep and not do a goddamm thing. After all, it wouldn't do any good to get to Manaus right away. Marlênio and Érica wouldn't be in the city until after Friday. At least that's what Pastor Edmundo had said.

The difference between the boat's first and second deck, where I was installed, in a hammock, was the air conditioning. Maybe, without Tiger, they'd have let me travel in first class, on the upper deck. But passengers with dogs weren't allowed there. Actually, they couldn't even get on the boat. I had to bribe the ticket seller.

On my level there were cabins with bunk beds and a dining room. The idea was not to mix the hammock people with the cabin people, or with those in the suites of the upper deck, but all the passengers ate there, in different shifts. And everybody ended up mingling on the deck, where there was a bar with music all day long.

I enjoyed seeing the tourists, listening to the gringos speak English. I think it was with Érica that I learned to be curious. I can't stand people who aren't interested in anything, she said. You know, insipid people with eyes like a dead fish? I hate it. Stupidity. I can't put up with it.

I don't know why I started thinking about that, but suddenly I remembered Érica crying, in her bikini, sitting on our bed.

I know very well what you do, she said, you kill for no reason, you kill for money.

Shut up, Érica, I shouted.

I won't shut up, you don't own me, she said, and she opened the wardrobe and started taking out her clothes. I'm leaving, she said, I've had it.

I got down on my knees. Don't do this to me, love. Don't abandon me.

But she wouldn't look at me. Then I went into the bathroom and rinsed my face. I came back, got my gun.

Unpack that suitcase, I said. Érica went pale. You're not leaving this apartment alive, I said. And if you do, I'll come after you, I'll find you, anywhere in the world, and kill you.

Now I was on that boat, carrying out what I'd promised Érica. Ten years later. The shitty part is that, when you're suffering, any thought is a trap. It doesn't matter what you're thinking; everything gets into your head, gets jumbled up, turns over and over, spins, and before you know it you're thinking about Érica.

That first day, as we were going up the Pará, the tourists were impressed by the houses on stilts. A lady said that in the state of Amazonas there was a hotel with 'the same concept' as those houses. I thought it was funny to call those rickety shacks a concept.

You get there, the woman said, explaining that she'd read it in the brochures at the hotel, and visit the homes of the backwoodsmen, see how they live, what they eat.

The poor backwoodsmen, commented a gringo with a funny-sounding accent.

He was German, I found out later, and had lived in Brazil for a long time. He had with him a pretty girl, much younger. Large dark eyes, long hair, she looked like an Indian.

Can you just imagine those people showing up and wanting to know what you eat? The gringo spoke softly, but I heard everything. Nair, he suggested, let's go sit on the other side.

Nair, I later discovered, was seventeen. She was always by herself, behind the German, who only wanted to read. He didn't pay any attention to her. All he did was read, the fool.

That's how the days went by. Most of the time I kept track of Nair. I liked seeing her sunbathe, what a lovely body, small, young. Sometimes I'd catch her looking at me too.

One day, she said hi to me. It was when I was trying to put Tiger on the wheeled cart. It wasn't working, and I was ready to give up.

The problem, she said, is that the dog isn't small and the cart is very low. You have to make an adaptation. Let's find some wood and screws. And a hammer.

I hate those things, but I went with Nair around the boat, asking for a hammer and a piece of wood, with Tiger limping and trying my patience. We were getting along fine, and then her boyfriend showed up.

Nair, he said, I've been looking all over the boat for you.

The long-haired guy was a real turn-off. For me and for Tiger. I finally gave up on the wheelchair for the dog, it was a lot of work. I'm not very good with a hammer, nails, that kind of thing. I threw everything in the river.

And Nair never said hi to me again, which made the trip a lot less interesting. Now and then, six, seven canoes would dock alongside us at the same time, like pirates, and the people would come on board, asking for things, selling flour, cheese, heart of palm.

The best time of day was at dawn. The deck was empty and you could stay there in peace. That's what I like. To keep quiet. To think about life. And piss in the river, instead of using those disgusting bathrooms. One of those times, I met Francisco. I liked his company, because it was like I was alone. He didn't talk, didn't ask questions, didn't make a sound. He followed me, somber, making no noise, not bothering me. And he played a good game of foosball. In the hold we discovered a table being shipped, and it was a good way to pass the time.

I don't remember when I noticed the bag. But it was at some stop before Santarém. Francisco wouldn't let it out of his sight. Not even to take a shower. He slept with it under his head. That's when I realized I was in danger. And that Francisco wasn't too smart. Neither was the guy who told him to follow me. I used to be in the business. That's not how the job was done.

I stole a sharp knife from the kitchen and started sleeping with one eye open.

Look here, you old hippie, I told Tiger, today you're going to suffer. You're going to walk a lot. You're going to get a lot of sun. You're going to see ugly things. But there's no choice. I can't leave you on the boat.

The stop in Santarém was for twelve hours, I'd been told. I already had a plan ready. A lot of tourists had gotten together to see the city, and I joined the group, taking the dog. It should be nice, I told Francisco. I'm going. It wasn't long before he came behind me.

Ashore, I was careful. The important thing was not to call attention to myself.

Nair looked beautiful that day, in green shorts and a white shirt.

What happened to the wheelchair for your dog? she asked.

It didn't work out, I said.

I wanted to talk more, say something, but her long-haired boyfriend didn't give me the chance, dragging Nair away, Let's go, Nair.

A driver was hired to take us to Alter do Chão and bring us back to the boat at the end of the day.

We all climbed into the rattletrap, some twenty people, and set out, wobbling, for the villa, eighteen miles away.

At the villa, we all went off in different directions, after telling the driver the time to return.

I spent the afternoon swimming, floating, thinking. The knife with me the whole time.

Francisco stayed at the beach with Tiger. Fully clothed. He didn't want to swim or drink beer. He was just there. Watching.

At lunchtime, I told Francisco I was going for a walk. I'm going to take a look at the river dolphins, I said. I made a point of letting him know I didn't want company. Tiger came after me, limping.

I hadn't gone ten steps before Francisco came after me. I'm going too, he said.

We plunged into the forest. The sun was grueling. I don't mind it a bit when a guy tries to get me from behind. In fact, I always thought it was a good way to die, you don't even know what hit you, bang, you die. But it's very unpleasant when the guy tries to be your friend before he kills you. Francisco was really pissing me off. Especially with that drivel of his.

We walked for over an hour.

You're sure it's here? he asked.

I looked around. Nobody. Tiger was tired. We sat down under a tree.

Francisco took off his shirt. Is it much further? he asked. I'm hungry.

I might not go back to the boat, I said.

He looked at me, surprised.

What about your baggage?

I don't have any, I said.

Francisco didn't even realize he was being tested. He didn't know what to do. Take out his weapon? Kill me right there?

He hesitated before acting. When he thought about opening the bag, I already had the knife at his throat.

Hand me the bag, I said.

Dude, he said, wait a minute.

The bag, I repeated.

He looked to the sides. There wasn't much he could do. He sighed and finally handed me the bag.

I opened it and dumped the contents on the ground: a gun, wallet, cellphone, keys. And a photo of me taken from a distance. Me and Tiger going into the hotel. My name was written on the back.

I took Francisco's papers from his wallet. Shit, the guy's name wasn't even Francisco.

The gun was loaded. A .38.

Máiquel, before you do something foolish, he said, I want to tell you what went down. I can explain everything. I'm going to talk, and not because you have a gun pointed at me.

I'm going to talk because I changed my mind, dude. We've become buddies.

Shit, the things you have to listen to when you're in charge of the situation.

The traitor Francisco said that Pastor Edmundo alerted Marlênio and Érica that I'd been at the church in Belém. The police had also been informed. So, they know you're heading for Manaus, he said. The police convinced Marlênio to stay in Manaus and give his talk in the city. They're going to use Marlênio as bait to catch you. That's the plan. They want you to think they don't know anything. But they're going to nab you the day you show up to see your daughter. Everything's set to go.

What else? I asked.

Marlênio doesn't agree with the police. That's where I came in. He sent me here to kill you. Marlênio's a chickenshit, he said, laughing.

I laughed too.

We can talk it out, he said. Those orders, we can change them. It can even work out the other way around. What comes here from there can just as well go there from here. Everything depends on the green, he said, laughing. I like you. We've become friends, he said. I have the names of Marlênio's contacts here. Everything's here, with me.

I hate people who switch sides. Those fuckers are scum. They infest the world. They dirty everything they touch. I pulled the trigger right there. Twice.

19

I threw his bag in the river but kept the revolver, the wallet with close to two thousand in it, and the cellphone without a battery.

I didn't manage to sleep anymore on the rest of the trip; sometimes I'd go down to the hold and stay there, crouching in a corner, going through the wallet of the traitor Francisco, whose real name was Éder and who was from Belém. Now he would rot in a shallow grave in Alter do Chão. Full of worms. That was another thing that robbed me of sleep, the grave. I should've dug it deeper. Soon the rain would leave the body exposed. The fishermen would discover it. The fishermen or some tourist.

It was very hot when I landed in Manaus. I stood there looking all around, behind me; I had long ago decided I'd never go back to jail.

At least in the port area, I noticed that the people don't

give a shit about the signs forbidding them from doing things. *No sleeping on rafts*, was written. *Be polite. Don't sit on the table. Don't put your feet on the bench. Don't spit on the raft.* That's all the signs said. People lodged on the tables, on the benches. Eating, sleeping. Spitting, I didn't see. But then I wasn't looking for it. I just wanted to get out of there as fast as possible.

I can show you around Manaus, said a girl with the features of an Indian and who couldn't have been more than fifteen. Hair dyed blonde. I didn't answer. In shorts and a top, swinging her hips, she explained that she knew Manaus like the palm of her hand. My name is Giane, she said.

How long are you going to be in the city? she wanted to know. I can take you to see everything. I'm good at that. Tourism, you know? We can do the city tour, know what that is? To get a general idea. See the Amazonas theater. The Adolpho Lisboa municipal market. Are you going to do any shopping?

I walked faster, trying to get rid of the girl. As I was about to get in the taxi, I saw that Tiger wasn't with me. Shit. Tiger, I shouted. He appeared, followed by the girl.

He was dying of thirst, she said, I gave him water. Do you know in what hotel you're staying? I know a very good one. Cheap. The Amazonas Palace. And they'll let you take the dog.

Let's go, I said.

Giane got into the car and gave the driver the address. I just love your dog, she said. When I was little –

That's where I stopped listening. I was watching the cars behind us. You've got to see everything, that's the rule. Who's in front, in back, to the sides. Because that's how you get caught. You relax, think everything's under control, and then, when you least expect it, somebody puts a bullet in your face.

I stayed in the shower until Giane returned with the things I'd asked her to buy, Merthiolate, Band-Aids, and a charger for the false Francisco's cellphone.

I put some money in her hand. You can go, I said.

You sure you don't want me to stay? she asked. After all, I'm already here.

I gave her fifty more to speed up the goodbye.

Can I at least take a shower? she asked. I'm dying from the heat.

While Giane bathed, I tested the device by calling Anderson.

The Bible-couple should already be there, he said. At the Hotel Veredas. Check it out, here's the phone number. I wrote it down. Marlênio himself gave Enir this information yesterday. Another thing: tomorrow there's going to be a meeting at Vivaldo Lima stadium, at two in the afternoon. Marlênio's going to speak. Know what they plan to announce at this convention? The construction of the largest evangelical temple in the world. They want to outdo the one already existing in Brazil, in Rio de Janeiro, if I'm not mistaken. They're going to show the model and all the rest. I hear the temple in Rio is unbelievable. It's a replica of Solomon's temple. What can be larger than Solomon's temple in Jerusalem? If we don't watch out, they're going to build a replica of the whole of Jerusalem. Can't you just picture it?

The information jibed with what Pastor Edmundo had said. I asked if Anderson knew someone who could sell me a silencer.

Piece of cake, he said. I'll get on it right away.

Do you think Marlênio has asked for police protection? I asked.

Of course, said Anderson. Unless he's stupid. Which he isn't, or he'd never have invented that God's card thing. He must've asked the police in Manaus for help.

I hung up and fell onto the bed. I was tired as shit.

Giane came out of the bathroom, wrapped in a towel.

Can I bandage your hand?

Put on some clothes first.

She went back into the bathroom and got dressed.

How'd you hurt yourself? she asked as she put Merthiolate on the palm of my hand.

Burying a body, I replied.

She thought it was funny. On the boat? You could've thrown the body in the river. It'd be a lot easier.

The fingertips were the worst part. Some of the nails had come loose.

I was hungry.

I asked Giane if she could bring me some pizza before she left. Get some for yourself too, I said, handing her the money.

Giane left and I listened to the noise from the hallway, the laughter, the conversations. And outside, the cars, the city. Shit. I hadn't slept in a bed for a long time. The smell of the sheets was good. The smell of detergent. Very good. Even more knowing the revolver was there, underneath the pillow.

The tiger shark has a bite like a can opener. It grinds, shreds, punctures everything it encounters, said the host. I opened my eyes and Giane was awake, eyes wide, watching the program. On the screen, a shark was circling, trying to attack sea lions that were scrambling onto the beach, one on top of the other.

That's why I hate swimming in the sea, said Giane. Those killers will eat anything. Even a car.

I looked at the clock, 3 a.m. I was real hungry, and there wasn't anything to eat in the room.

I've seen a program about detectives and one about chimps, said Giane. Did you know that chimps like to kill for the fun of it?

There's still a slice of pizza that I bought yesterday, said Giane. You were asleep when I got here. Tiger's a big eater, he ate everything.

Let's go out, I said.

We went to an all-night restaurant that Giane was familiar with and ordered grilled fish.

Eat this ground manioc, it's typical of here, Giane insisted. Mix it with the fish sauce and swallow. Don't chew. Put pepper on it. Delicious, isn't it?

The only problem with Giane was that she talked too much. She made me dizzy.

I showed her the brochure Pastor Edmundo had given me. I asked about the Hotel Veredas.

It's a rich man's hotel. It's downtown, not far from here.

What about the Vivaldo Lima stadium?

It's on Avenida Constantino Nery. Why?

I need to go there, I said.

You're weird, she said. What did you come to Manaus to do?

To look for some people.

Who?

You talk too much.

She laughed, embarrassed.

After eating, we took a taxi and drove past the stadium.

You want me to stop here? the driver said, wary.

Just drive around it, I replied.

I also asked him to go by the Veredas. Slowly, I said. Very slowly.

I looked at everything, saw a van in front of the hotel. They must've already arrived.

Can I stay here with you? Giane asked when we arrived back at the Amazonas Palace. I'll leave tomorrow. It's 'cause I live a long way from here. It's easier.

You can have the bed, I said. I spread the blanket on the floor and went to sleep beside Tiger.

Giane had a funny way of waking up, like someone had turned on a switch, really good-humored. Hi, everything okay? Sleep well? Do you remember what you dreamt about?

Shit. Never saw anything like it.

Can I ask you something? she said. Do you think I'm ugly? You can tell the truth.

You're pretty.

I'm too thin. I know that. Tell the truth. I don't mind.

The false Francisco's cellphone rang. It might be Marlênio asking if I was dead. He must be curious to know how I died. On what beach my body was rotting. I'm alive, that's what I'd tell him when he called. On the boat I'd given that phone call a lot of thought. I was going to answer and say his plan hadn't worked. I killed the false Francisco, I was going to say. And I took his money. And his revolver. I'm in Manaus, I was going to say. Very close by. You'd better disappear. Because if I find you, you won't get away. That's what I was going to tell him. You're fucked, I was going to say. And even if you disappear it won't do much good. Because I've got nothing better to do than to go after you. You're my favorite sport. My other enemies, I was going to say, are all dead. I killed them myself. You're the only one left. That's what I'd thought about saying. But suddenly, when the phone rang, I changed my mind. I decided not to answer. Even if it was Marlênio. I didn't have anything to say to that piece-of-shit preacher. Not even Fuck you. I didn't want to hear a word of what he had to say. Let him be in the dark. That was the game. Each of us in his corner. After so many years, the thing was coming down to the wire. No words. I just wanted to bring it to an end. It was a matter of closure. Kill him, that was all.

I turned off the phone and got dressed. I told Giane I had to go to work.

I'm too bony, that's my problem, isn't it?

You're fine, I said.

What about my teeth? Do you think they jut out?

No, I answered. You're just right. Close the door when you leave.

Giane was very skinny. Bony. A pinched face. But I wasn't going to tell her that. There are some things you can't say to a woman.

I got on a bus and went to the Grande Fortuna shanty town, outside of Manaus.

That's the best price I can give you, said Chicão, putting the pistol and silencer in my lap. Take it or leave it. I'm making you a good price because I try to accommodate people who come highly recommended.

Chicão was a guard at the Manaus penitentiary. He made four hundred a month, but his real money came from selling guns to the prisoners. On the kitchen table at his house were two brand-new power drills. A special order from the inmates. He tried to convince me to help. I'll make you an even better price if you come along, he said. A real winner, that guy.

I bought the silencer and the pistol and left.

On the way back, I bought a pizza at a bar near the hotel.

I found Giane in the bed.

I decided to wait for you, she said. I felt bad about leaving Tiger alone.

What about your family? Do you have anywhere to go?

I'm of age.

Show me your ID.

I'm going to be eighteen. A week from now.

I sat down on the bed and began fitting the silencer. Lying girl. I liked the pistol.

I glanced to the side and saw Giane with her head between her hands, skinny, she looked like a blonde mouse. I felt affection for her.

What's the problem at home? I asked. You have a father?

She didn't answer.

You can stay here as long as you like, I said. I mean, until I leave.

Before five, I got into the shower with Tiger. Soap and water didn't do any good. Even clean he stank. He would come out of the bath and already start to stink. Must be because of his ugliness, poor thing.

I rubbed his paws, his tail, his ears, dried him thoroughly and put some deodorant on his coat.

I went back to the shower and took my bath. I hadn't shaved for two weeks. I left the hotel and went to a barber shop. I asked for a goatee. And to have my head shaved. Right down to the scalp, I said.

Afterward, I bought a beret and dark glasses.

I like it, Giane said when I returned. You look like some old rocker. All that's missing is the leather jacket. And the pot belly.

The smell of green corn paste made me nauseous, the way Giane scarfed it down first thing in the morning turned my stomach. I'm way too skinny, she said. All I could swallow was a little coffee.

Afterwards, we went back to the room and watched TV, killing time.

At 1 p.m. we took a bus to the stadium.

What are we going to do there? Giane asked, holding my hand.

We're going to find some people, I said.

En route, she told me she lived with her mother and stepfather. He had beaten her, and that's why she didn't want to go home. The guy is a bastard. I'd much rather live with you, she said.

I didn't even answer.

I think I'm in love with you.

I pretended not to hear, I went on looking at the city.

I'm serious, she continued. I'll soon be sixteen. Want to see my ID?

She stuck the ID card in my face. She still had six months to go before she was sixteen, that's what I saw.

I'm crazy about you, she said.

We remained silent the rest of the way.

Let's go, I said, when we got to the stadium.

Holding hands, we passed by a police van.

I bought two T-shirts. JESUS LOVES YOU, they said. Put this on, I said.

A group of evangelicals was getting out of a van. I took advantage and went in with them.

In the stadium, there were other cops. Marlênio's people, maybe. I tried to remember what it was like when the guys would hire me and my boys to handle their security. We would say yes, we protected, set up a plan, promise things. But the truth is simple. Nobody can provide one hundred per cent security. Plans are full of holes.

I went in through the main door. With the pistol in Giane's purse. No one paid any attention to me. I might even have been good. But more likely, they were shitty at their job.

20

The girls in white on stage jumped around, fat, *Only Christ saves*, they sang, with rolls of blubber at their waists, held out their arms, *I shall go with Christ*, they would take a step forward, together, happy, a step back, then they'd jump again, that band of fatties, and the crowd in the stands, on the grass followed their movements, crossing their hands on their chests, throwing their arms into the air, always singing, *It's time to obey, Only Jesus can save us*. Only me and Giane didn't know how to dance. At least move your arms, said Giane, and then a mulatto pastor came on stage and started making funny; nothing irritates me more than those guys trying to be comical.

I am very happy, he said, to be able to introduce Jesus to those who have not yet had personal contact with Christ.

Shit, what a laugh. These guys visited the house of Christ like someone going to the bakery. Christ is their buddy. What a clown. That went on for a very long time.

Afterwards, a large screen descended, and the plan for the new temple, which would be built in Brasilia, was projected onto it.

It will be the largest evangelical temple in the world, said the mulatto, yelling so much that he looked like he was possessed.

I was already dizzy. Let's go down, I told Giane.

We left the stands and joined the crowd on the grass.

We took our inspiration, brethren, from the second temple of Solomon, built by the Hebrews and destroyed in 70 AD. On the screen, drawings appeared. Do you know what remains of it, brethren? Only the eastern wall, and it is from that wall that we have brought to you, and here it is, in my hands, the stone that will be the cornerstone of our construction.

Every time he said the word 'stone', some kind of trumpet would sound, and the crowd would howl.

Here it is, brethren. The stone. Look upon it, for it is the beginning of everything.

I didn't see anything. A tiny little rock and they raised such a big stink over it, this time with one of those songs they play for car races on television.

The temple of Solomon, my brethren, was burned by the Romans, by the barbarians, by the Italians, the Catholics, but we are here, and we shall rebuild the Promised Land.

Rejoice, brethren, for our temple will rise from the ashes, he said, from the ashes, by the power of God. Here, beginning with this stone.

We stayed there for a long time, several preachers were

introduced, it was no different from what you see on TV. Besides the music, there were attractions, mutilated people, the lame, cripples, telling how their lives improved after they found Jesus. They brought the faithful to the stage, a voodoo follower who converted, a marriage saved, a bar owner who'd gone bankrupt because of the Devil and later recovered everything.

Only then did Marlênio appear. Different from the others, he stayed further back on stage longer. And always protected by female helpers; he was afraid, the bastard. A wide-eyed stare. Using women as a shield.

What will our temple of Solomon be used for? It will be our energy. Our light. It will orient us so we can build a future. And future, in our Church, means sowing love. By building churches throughout the world. Because what we have just heard here is a portrait in miniature of the strength, the power, of our missionary work. We can be much more. And we need much more.

I noticed that, in front of the stage, in the center and at the sides, was a large number of men. They must be police.

Brazil needs our help, said Marlênio. God has given us this mission. Do you know the increase in the suicide rate in the south of the country? Almost thirty-one per cent. Because there we've had a record growth in spiritism and voodoo. That is our challenge. And we're going to put an end to that. We're going to build churches in that region. We're going to conquer those hearts.

He said that and took a step back. Impossible to hit his head from there. I'd have to climb onto the stage.

We must preach the Gospel in this country. Atheism has grown three hundred and fifty per cent in Brazil in recent years.

Another step back. Damn. Soon he'd be leaving by the rear of the stage.

We have a public to reach. Children. Adolescents. Indians. It is they who are farthest from Jesus.

Let's go, I told Giane. I wasn't going to be able to do anything there.

I want that one there, I told the vendor, pointing to a black Volks parked at the front of the rental agency. I paid in advance and drove away. Giane, barefoot, her feet on the dashboard, was quiet.

I liked going there, she said. I got a good feeling from the music. Did you hear that man saying how he used to be lost? A slave of the Devil? You think he's happy, Máiquel?

Beats me, I said.

He said he was, he insisted on it.

Do you believe, she asked after a time, that a hairy snake came out of his dick?

That was one of the stories we'd heard, that the Devil was trying to end some guy's marriage. I was disgusted by my wife, the man said, and me by him, said the woman, until the day a hairy snake came out of his penis.

It was a serpent, a serpent, repeated the mulatto preacher, behold what the Devil does to people, and yet there are those who still do not believe.

I don't think they were lying, said Giane. Why would they lie to us?

I parked the car a short distance from the entrance to the hotel.

I took the pistol from Giane's purse, told her to wait for me in the car, and got out. There was a police van, I noticed. But the policeman was dozing at the steering wheel.

The entrance to the Hotel Veredas was enormous. A lot of people wandering around, children, groups of tourists; in an hour Marlênio would be coming through there, I thought. I picked up a newspaper, sat on a sofa and stuck my face in it. *Deadly Games. Terror. Showing at the Amazonas 3. Dogfight. Action. Cinemark 8. Real estate. House for sale. Good location. Living room. Dining room. Two bedrooms. Contact Jerônimo.*

Suddenly, the policeman who was sleeping came in. He crossed the lobby toward the swimming pool. *Wanted: apartment or house in any part of Manaus. Contact Geisa.*

I saw that the lobby had a booth with smoked glass for anyone wanting to use the computer. I went in, the place was perfect. I could see who was coming in, going out, and still I was well hidden. But then a tourist appeared and started waiting to get on the machine. I pretended I was using the computer. After a time, he gave up.

The policeman came back across the lobby, said something to the receptionist, and returned to the front of the hotel.

Ten minutes later, somebody else wanted to use the computer. As soon as I saw her coming, I turned my back to the door and started typing.

I'm going to be some time, I said.

Excuse me, but you have to write in the password, she said.

The girl had opened the door to the booth to tell me this. I was about to explode, shit, what a pushy girl, but when I turned around I saw it was Samantha.

At the reception desk, she said, they have tokens for ten and twenty minutes.

And then she saw my T-shirt, with the name of the event I'd just returned from. JESUS LOVES YOU.

My father is a pastor, she said. He was there today too.

I wasn't able to say anything. My face was like stone.

Do you want to use my password? she asked. I can get another.

Samantha didn't give me time to answer. She typed her password in the computer, expertly, fast, and I could smell her scent very close, full of chlorine from the pool, the smell of a rich little girl.

Now, she said, all you have to do is click on Internet Explorer, here.

Shit, I didn't understand a thing of what she was saying.

Samantha saw my stupid expression.

You can use it now, she said.

I'm waiting for my friend, I said.

She didn't understand. But aren't you going to use it?

Yes. In a little while.

She waited for me to do something. But I couldn't move. Or say anything.

I'm going to go into Hotmail, she said.

She talked like her mother. She had the same voice. It was like I was hearing Cledir. But what really knocked me out was her hands. On the keyboard. They were a copy of mine. Identical. The thumb. The pinky.

Samantha, said a woman, I've been looking for you, your mother's calling.

Ciao, she said.

I watched her move away. At the rear of the lobby, in a wraparound and a bikini, was Érica. Hair wet, shit, Érica. My legs went rubbery. Érica and Samantha headed toward the pool. I waited a bit and went after them. I watched everything from a distance. Shit, Érica. So near, all I had to do was go over there, that was all. Such a long time. Now there she was, two seconds away. There used to be times when I would stand motionless, waiting for something to happen. Anything. That day, looking at Érica, I experienced that sensation. I couldn't move, I was like stone, not breathing, with the feeling that if I moved I'd ruin something. I don't know what, they were just eating a sandwich. Shit. Érica was fucking beautiful. I don't know why I remembered a game we used to play. I'd see a guy in a toupee and say, Érica, I'll pay you five bills to go over there and yank that rug off his head. I'll pay you five bills if you kiss that woman on the back of the neck, you kiss her and ask her pardon, you didn't mean to, and we'd laugh like crazy about it. We would walk leisurely, fooling around, and I would sometimes tease Érica, imitating her way of talking, gawdammit, dawg, and she'd shove me, You fool, there's nothing uglier than a São Paulo accent, you don't pronounce your s's, you idiot. Stupid thing, our thoughts. The things you remember.

Érica helped Samantha with her sandwich, stuck a straw in her glass, chatted with the girl. Then I saw her cross the lobby, by herself, while Samantha stayed with the other woman. Érica went to the computer booth. She saw there was no one there. She looked around. Spoke to someone at the reception desk. And went back to the pool. She was worried. Then I saw her take Samantha by the hand and go into the elevator.

It was 4.30 when Marlênio got to the hotel. He was accompanied by two bruisers, but they didn't come in with him, they stayed outside with the policeman who was already there.

If I should ever set up a new security agency, two things were for sure: never hire policemen, 'cause they're all corrupt and lazy. They do a shitty job. And in addition I'd never get someone to act as bodyguard, I'd do it myself. Nobody knows how to do it right. Just imagine, letting the guy come into the hotel by himself. Just because there's a cop at the door? What are they thinking? That killers punch a time clock?

Marlênio went to the reception desk, and I went to the jewelry store.

The elevator opened, a pasty-white couple got out. From where I was, looking through the mirrors in the display window, I saw everything. A lady went into the elevator. A plump woman with two children also got in, but Marlênio wasn't in time to go up with the pack. He had to wait for the next elevator. He stood there in his three-piece suit, sweating, loosening his tie, probably sensing something. He must have thought about calling the bruisers, but there was no reason to, because I was hidden behind a column, in the jewelry store. He looked toward the reception desk, toward the door. And then, a young woman showed up. I never paid the slightest attention to such things, but at that moment I remembered the voodoo priest who told me to tattoo a star on my dick. To seal your body, he said. Prick-star, I thought, seal everything here. Put an end to this shit. Send everybody away, because this is between the two of us, me and that man. And then another person arrived. Shit. To really fuck things up. A little girl. Marlênio was right beside them. The elevator door opened, Marlênio got in, and the child came running out. Her mother came after her. They must have smelled shit.

The elevator was already closing when I pushed the button again and got in. Marlênio, shit, it was funny to see the face he made. He tried to get out. He tried to push the alarm bell, but my body was in the way. I was the one pushing the buttons here.

Máiquel, he said as the elevator started to climb, Samantha – but I didn't let him finish.

I didn't know anything about Samantha. But he wasn't going to be the one to tell me. I put two bullets in his belly. Blood spattered all over the mirror.

When the door opened on the fifth floor, I understood everything. Samantha was there, waiting for Marlênio. And me with the gun in my hand.

I stuck the weapon in my pocket. Shit. Blood was starting to soak the preacher's shirt.

Samantha, I said.

She withdrew a step.

I grabbed the upright ashtray from the corridor to prop open the elevator door. Samantha, I said, I wanted to tell her everything, explain, that guy, I said, that man, I wanted to say everything calmly, say many things, speak of the time when I sold cars and was married to Cledir, but at that moment, shit, everything was already ruined, everything lost, I felt confused. Do you know who I am, Samantha? I continued, taking a step forward, and then she ran off down the hall, I ran after her, both of us running, and that was when I realized that Marlênio had fucked me for ever.

We came to Apartment 514 almost together. Samantha clung to Érica, and I locked the bedroom door. That was the worst part. The three of us there. After so much time. Together. Everything finished. And the way the two of them looked at me. That was what enraged me, the way they stared at me. Like I was the Devil.

I asked Érica what Samantha knew. About us two. There was no way to ask about Cledir.

Lord God, Érica began, placing her hand on Samantha's head.

I had so many things to ask, soon Marlênio's body would be discovered there, I was in a hurry, and Érica wouldn't stop praying, wouldn't answer me.

In the name of Thy Son Jesus Christ, she said, I beg help for my daughter, bless the life of my little girl.

Shit, answer what I'm asking you, I said. You went away, Érica, you went away and took my daughter, I said, and even

212

worse, Samantha started praying too, begging God to deliver her from evil.

Samantha, I said, no one's going to hurt you.

Shit, she didn't even hear, I got so fucking mad I couldn't stand still, I went to the window. Then I opened the outer door to see if Marlênio's body was still there.

Érica, I said, God can't save you. Only I can save you now.

But the two went on praying and ignoring me.

I keep thinking, I said, what would you do if I took Samantha with me now? If I disappeared from the map? Me and Samantha. Taking all your money. What do you think of that idea, Érica?

You two ruined everything, you and Marlênio.

Samantha wouldn't look at me. There was nothing more that could be done. Never again.

Before locking the two in the bathroom, I smashed the telephone.

Then I went down the service stairway and out the front entrance. The bruisers were there, having a friendly conversation with the policeman, while Marlênio was bleeding like a pig in the elevator.

When I got to the car, Giane was asleep. I went straight to my hotel.

I paid the bill, put Tiger in the car, in the back seat.

What about me? Giane asked, on the sidewalk.

I don't know.

Her expression turned crappy.

Don't cry, I said. I can't take you with me.

That's all I needed, staying there, wasting time, seeing the girl cry, while the cops were after me. Shit, they must already be on their way.

I didn't want to know. I'm a fugitive. I turned my back and got into the car.

ALSO AVAILABLE BY PATRÍCIA MELO
INFERNO

For eleven-year-old Kingie, there are lessons to be learned from drug trafficking. His first job is as a lookout, working on the hillside slums of Rio de Janerio. But as he grows older he realises that in order to survive you must also keep a close watch on yourself as well. In *Inferno* Patrícia Melo tells of Kingie's life of crime, of his poverty-ridden childhood, how he pursues his dreams and the way he learns to achieve leadership. In his uncertain world, chaos manifests itself as violence and deprivation, whether machine-gun fire, unwanted adolescent pregnancy, or the fraught relationships between servants and their employers. Kingie's path intersects with a network of stories of love, family, crime and power. The plot twists through a compelling tale where rapid-fire language and a sharp sense of humour combine to make this gripping story.

*

'Tarantino meets Benigni … this is a novel that grabs you by the guts
– then rests uneasily on your mind'
INDEPENDENT ON SUNDAY

'A gritty, exciting and sometimes harrowing tale of life
on the mean streets of Rio de Janeiro'
INDEPENDENT

*

ISBN 9780747561590 · PAPERBACK · £6.99

B L O O M S B U R Y

BLACK WALTZ

A successful and renowned conductor of a major symphony orchestra in São Paulo is married to a beautiful and talented violinist close to thirty years his junior. But his happiness is undermined by two fears: that he will never wholly share her life because, unlike her, he is not Jewish; and that she will be unfaithful to him. Jealousy – beyond the reach of reason – haunts his every moment, gnawing at his trust, his love, and ultimately his sanity. *Black Waltz* opens a fascinating and harrowing window into a mind bordering on paranoia and psychosis.

*

'A white-knuckle read'
GUARDIAN

'A cruelly focused, finely balanced and brilliantly written study.
Her great achievement is to make what, on the surface, is a simple tale
of a man's jealousy and mid-life doubt, into a swelling epic of
grubby emotion and deep, empty despair'
SUNDAY HERALD

'The study of a man's disintegration into pathological jealousy ...
the novel speeds along'
TIMES LITERARY SUPPLEMENT

*

ISBN 9780747576594 · PAPERBACK · £7.99

ORDER YOUR COPY: BY PHONE +44 (0)1256 302 699; BY EMAIL: DIRECT@MACMILLAN.CO.UK
DELIVERY IS USUALLY 3–5 WORKING DAYS. FREE POSTAGE AND PACKAGING FOR ORDERS OVER £20.

ONLINE: WWW.BLOOMSBURY.COM/BOOKSHOP
PRICES AND AVAILABILITY SUBJECT TO CHANGE WITHOUT NOTICE.

WWW.BLOOMSBURY.COM/PATRICIAMELO

B L O O M S B U R Y